About Flying
No. 11
2024

Managing Editor:	Steve Lindahl
Poetry Editor:	Mary Hennessy
Non-Fiction Editor:	Jennifer Stevenson Vincent
Fiction Editor:	Howard Pearre
Fiction Readers:	Joni Carter Ray Morrison Steve Lindahl
Cover Art:	Barbara Rizza Mellin

Flying South is a literary magazine/writing contest published annually by Winston-Salem Writers, an association of writers and readers with the purpose of:

Building community and helping writers improve their craft.

Information about Winston-Salem Writers can be found at the website: **www.wswriters.org**

Winston-Salem Writers is a non-profit organization and a partner with The Arts Council of Winston-Salem and Forsyth County, NC.

Friends of Flying South

Thank you for your generous donations!

Craige Jenkins Liipfert & Walker LLP
Attorneys at Law

The attorneys at **Craige Jenkins Liipfert & Walker LLP** take pride in providing specialized advice in all areas of family and corporate law.

* * *

Mae Lipscomb Rodney has degrees in library science from North Carolina Central University and the University of North Carolina at Chapel Hill. In 2015 the UNC School of Information and Library Science celebrated her extended career by naming her the Distinguished Alumna of the Year. She has written several short plays including *Zelda is Dead*, *Black Diamonds*, and *India's Story*. In addition, she has compiled multiple biographies. She is a member of Winston-Salem's Black Philanthropy Initiative, Women's Fund board of directors, Winston-Salem Foundation's Racial Equity Advocates. Mae currently serves as secretary on the board of Winston-Salem Writers.

Contents

2024 Third Place Winners:

Fiction:

Creative Nonfiction:

Poetry:

Susan Woods Morse

Joyce Schmid

Aborted Grief

Rebecca Petzel

Twenty-three weeks and one day into my third pregnancy I almost died. There was no warning, no earlier signs that this pregnancy could be complicated or dangerous.

One moment I was perfectly healthy and inching day-by-day towards the 24 week viability line, a date my midwives shared during my previous pregnancy as one to circle on the calendar — as The Day after which the little growing being inside me would have a chance to survive in the outside world.

The next moment I was struck with blinding, unbearable pain curled up on the bathroom floor.

I'd heard stories of people dying of heart attacks in the bathroom alone. They're with their families, at work, or an event. Suddenly they feel ill, or off. Embarrassed to be vulnerable and in pain with others, they slink off to a bathroom to compose themselves… and die alone. These stories flashed into my mind when after an urge to use the restroom, I was suddenly doubled over by pain. I slipped off the toilet seat down into the fetal position and released a gutteral scream for my husband — hoping against hope he was home and could hear my cries — overwhelmed with the certainty that whatever was happening was real, and I did not want to die alone in the bathroom afraid to be vulnerable.

Relief flooded through my body when I heard my husband's foot steps pounding down the stairs; I moaned 'thank you' when his figure appeared above me in the doorway. And yet after he quickly joined me on the bathroom floor, begging me to tell him what was wrong, my certainty at the seriousness of the moment started to waver. As I struggled to explain my distress, my mind filled with familiar self-doubt, thinking "Don't be so dramatic, it can't be that bad." I'm glad I called for help before the "you can't trust what you feel" voices started to mumble. And I'm glad my husband didn't have those same voices in his head, at least not right then, as I was quickly trying to convince us both that everything was fine.

However by then I was also bleeding, profusely. Bleeding that put my 'miscarriage at eight weeks' bleeding from three years earlier to shame. And every time I tried to move I was sick. So my husband called 911 for help to get me and the 23 weeks and 1 day old fetus growing inside of me to the hospital.

*

The only thing I remember about the time between collapsing in a pool of sick and blood in my hallway during a failed attempt to move towards the front door, and being in the ambulance with the paramedics, is the calm, submissive, scared oversight of my normally exuberant and out of control cattle dog mutt. Her uncharacteristic fear and stillness in that moment would haunt me for weeks. Wondering if my two year old and his daycare friends who spent their days in our yard had seen me on that stretcher covered in blood, similarly muted of their normal carefree bouncing exuberance, also haunted me.

By the time the paramedics were unloading my stretcher at the hospital, the "be rational, be calm, don't be so anxious" voices in my head had completely won the day and I was ashamed of my need for ambulance support. Instead of fearing for my own life, my self-doubt and I had figured out a new, much more obvious explanation for the moment: I was losing the pregnancy and needed to prepare to say goodbye to my baby. From what I'd deduced listening to the paramedics and ER staff, I was on the verge of delivering a 23 week and 1 day old baby four months before his due date, and six days before the "call us after 24 weeks" viability line advertised on the midwives business card.

But of course, it wasn't that simple. Through a fog of triage room medical chaos, I came to understand that in fact I was about to deliver a baby on the very first day of an in-between period, what the doctor described as "the worst possible time for this to be happening to you. I'm so sorry." It turns out 23 weeks is *probably* not viable for a baby to survive outside the womb, and if viable almost certainly (but not definitely) would result in major life complications. We were somewhere between the heartbreaking certainty of a 22 week delivery which would automatically be a miscarriage (or abortion depending on the circumstances), and the medical systems clarity about a 24 week delivery, where the doctors at my state hospital in Illinois were required by law to do everything possible to save a baby if delivered, deeming those they can't save no longer miscarried but stillborn. And everyone who was supporting me and the baby needed to know what to do if he was born during this medically and legally ambiguous window. Should we fight to save our baby through this trauma whatever complications may come? Or should we call it a loss and move on in life without him? There were Life and Death and all the grey in between decisions to be made. And it was up to us.

Now my "be rational" voices had work to do. It was time to quiet the feelings, the fear and grief at losing this baby. I needed to be smart, to talk to the doctors, the midwives, and nurses. It was time to study. And it was urgent. This was happening now.

At least "now" in the relative terms of labor and delivery. Even in dire circumstances, babies don't transition from in utero to outside quickly.

*

All night doctors from the NICU came in and out of our room on the fourth floor of the old brutalist-era hospital building — navigating to my bedside past what felt like the hospital's entire labor and delivery staff — to help us understand neonatal biological systems, the chances of traumatic damage to each of those systems in the coming hours, miraculous NICU technological advancements, and what it was like to meet an only 23 week developed baby. I willed myself to stay focused as I listened, trying to ignore the ongoing gushes of blood tended to by a nurse who diligently weighed and replaced the blood-soaked piles of hospital chucks lining my bed.

The weight of the blood I lost wasn't my concern; it was someone else's job to make sure I didn't run out. Mine was to figure out instructions for what to do when we meet the baby. Fight like hell to save him despite what sounded like unsurmountable odds? Or give him a graceful death? Would we want to hold him whether he is born dead or alive? Provide palliative pain relief if he's strong enough to take a breath? If he cries on his own, should we throw palliative care out the window and take that as a declaration to fight? If we decide to resuscitate the baby after birth, can we change our minds if it all goes terribly wrong? What is our understanding of neonatal suffering and feeling and souls and will and choice?

Approximately eight hours, one full work day, into the highest stakes study course of my life — during which my medical team directed countless blood draws, blood transfusions, worked to address my collapsing veins, administered medicines to help me, and medicines to help the baby — an OBGYN resident I've come to call "glasses" sat down at my bedside. Today, with the experience of many months in the hospital system, I know that a doctor sitting down in a chair to talk to you is not a harbinger of good news. At the time all I knew was I loved her green tortoise shell glasses and what a calming, kind presence she was as I tried to stay connected to my crash course on palliative neonatal care, while keeping the intense fear and pain and generally *not good* sensations coursing through my body at bay.

Focusing in on her face as I laid huddled in the fetal position — now on my right side after the herculean effort of countless nurses to move my failing body into some position, any position, where I could bear the pain — she calmly said "I'm worried about you, you're not doing well." And in that instant I tapped back into my body, this feeling, once again, that I was dying.

I'd known it was a possibility this whole time. You don't meticulously watch a team of nurses and doctors setting up four different IV lines, trying to project calmness while they keep reiterating "STAT" on all their orders, without knowing it's a possibility. I'd spent hours responsibly and not hysterically telling everyone who would listen that if at any point there was a choice to make I'd appreciate if they would "please prioritize my life, I would like to survive this." I thought to myself all evening how grateful I was to live in a time and place where I felt confident they would follow that directive and not jeopardize my life for a dogma or a stigma.

But there is a difference between rationally knowing death is a possibility, and realizing that dying is indeed what your body is in the process of doing. I suspect this conversation with glasses wasn't the first time someone in my very busy labor and delivery room said the words DIC. But staring at her calm face as she spoke was the first time I understood that the blood condition I was experiencing — disseminated intravascular coagulation (DIC) — as a result of massive blood loss, was in the words of my neighbor "game over." And despite the countless pokes and medicines and everything else the medical team were doing to care for me over the last eight hours, I was still in DIC. "Your blood is consuming itself," she explained, a sentence to this day I can't comprehend. But I understood the cooler full of blood they'd ordered to the hallway right outside our door, preparing for the next hail mary step to save my life: a mass transfusion event where machines constantly circulate blood for me.

I did not want to go there. Nobody wanted to go there.

It was time to actively force out the presumed cause of all this bleeding — our 23 week and 1 day old baby. Because while I was in graduate school studying neonatology and the probability of survival alongside quality of life considerations, dilation had reversed and delivery had gone from momentarily imminent to stalled. And despite the still astounding levels of pain I was experiencing, there were no longer signs the baby was on his way out. In fact all the signs pointed to him being healthy and content to remain on the inside despite the torrents of blood surrounding his protective water sac. I imagined him floating around with a totally normal heart rate, chill as can be, enjoying all the new hospital sounds to decipher as we'd learned he was just in the process of developing his hearing.

There are no perfectly safe ways to deliver a 23 week old baby. Their malleable skulls, their not yet developed skin, their completely insufficient lungs and digestive system. The trauma of birth this undeveloped is often a death sentence. But if you want to give them a fighting chance, you cut them out via the sunroof to avoid squishing their brains through the birth canal and the (almost guaranteed) brain bleeding a vaginal birth causes. However you do not cut into the belly of a woman in DIC whose blood is failing, as that is a certain death sentence for another soul. And so amidst the crowd of specialists who had been working together all night to keep me and this baby alive, the doctor from the family planning team stepped forward to help us plan the abortion of our baby. This was the dead-end destination of the "if there's a choice to make, please prioritize my life" path we'd selected. We signed all the consent forms to give our doctors permission to act to the best of their ability to save my life and treat what I was sure would be the baby's fleeting life on the outside with care and dignity in the process of termination. We all wanted to give the baby a chance, but from what I'd gleaned during neonatology 101 the past eight hours, there wasn't much of a chance for our baby after all we'd been through.

This was goodbye.

*

It was around six a.m. when the foley balloon was set to re-dilate my cervix and the abortion was in progress. After I'd sent the handful of "just in case I die" text messages that felt necessary, and the nurses activated another blood transfussion, the room finally cleared and my husband and I were alone with nothing to decide for the first time since I'd been admitted to the hospital the day before.

And I finally cried.

I sobbed, viscerally shaking with the grief of it all. My husband crawled gently next to me in bed and held me as the weight of everything that had changed inexplicably on the drop of a dime washed over me. But only for a moment, a very brief moment, what felt like mere seconds, before another nurse came in to check my blood levels. And it was time to pull myself together and do everything I could to make the hospital's job of saving my life — and ending my baby's — as easy as possible. I wouldn't want to burden these kind, hard working people, doing the best they could in a terrible situation, with something as unbearable as my grief.

*

Every thirty minutes a nurse came in to draw blood and run labs to continue directing my lifesaving treatment. Otherwise, we waited. It turns out abortions aren't fast, either.

Then a few hours later, everything changed. Again. My DIC numbers started to rebound and the rate of bleeding finally slowed. With my life no longer on the line we were offered the chance to end the abortion, and while holding our breath at the precarious inexplicability of it all, we seized the moment.

Nobody in my hospital had ever seen or heard of a pregnancy continuing after a mother entered DIC. They knew of mothers surviving DIC... but not still pregnant. Our shared survival remains a medical mystery. By now I've learned not to pick too much at this mystery, as it doesn't seem to help a thing. I will never know what saved us. All I know is that this particular day was not the end for one or the other or both of us. But instead the start of the fight to save the baby we ultimately named Ori. The fight to hear his first cry when he joined us in the outside world eighteen critical days later. To keep him alive through a tumultuous three and a half month neonatal ICU hospitalization; to keep every flu and cold and deadly omicron variant of the coronavirus away from our vulnerable, ventilated tiny-baby. To introduce him to his big brother when we brought him home 120 days after the fight began. To pretend the work of it all wasn't ripping our family apart at the seams; that I was strong enough, we were all strong enough, for the work at hand.

Meanwhile — all that unfelt grief for the baby I knew I'd lost, all the sadness and confusion and overwhelm of feeling my own life slip away, remained politely bottled up and pushed down; a terrified force whose feelings seemed no longer relevant. It was time to be grateful. We survived. Be rational. We were the lucky ones, we'd come so close to the brink that we understood our good fortune more intimately than most. Why did we survive? "It's just random math," one doctor proclaimed. The math that at first was against us, that turned our lives upside down in a moment, was now for us. "What on earth do you have to be sad about, this story has a happy ending" the "be rational" voices scolded in my brain, while that unbearably heavy and still unseen grief, that was never invited to the table, burrowed deeper and deeper inside.

Piedmonters

Mason Boyles

I'm taking a midnight lap around my apartment complex when someone stumbles out from behind the dumpsters and scares the melatonin out of me.

"Mothersucker," she says. Jaylin.

I rub my face to make sure it's attached.

"I'll come to you," she tells me.

She's twice as tall as last time I saw her, swallowed in an orange windbreaker that feels like the product of an unidentifiable phase. She still runs like her limbs are trying to escape from her torso. You get older, you grow, but you move the same way.

She steps under streetlight I've backed into. Her cheeks look like the skin on your stomach, if that makes sense. When we were younger, I used to think that was what was wrong with her: she had all the right parts to be a person, but the order was wrong.

"Spooked me."

"Just wait." She fishes out a photo folded longways.

I know what it shows before she opens it. "You saved them?"

"I found them. The real people."

Who'd haunted our fort half a decade ago. I can see their smirks on the backs of my shut eyelids: the bald guy and steeple-eyebrowed wife and their weirdly trapezoidal offspring.

"Behind the Exxon off Monkey Junction," Jaylin's saying. "Come lay eyes, Bailey."

I open mine and she's bouncing on her toes like a bantamweight. Three hydrangea leaves are pinched in her windbreaker's zipper.

"It's witching hour."

"You're awake." She drags me behind the dumpsters to where her Mom's doorless Jeep is rusting. "Just let me know I'm not crazy," she says. "Please."

We'd been friends in the mindless way that happens when you're eleven and neighbors. This was the summer my parents moved to Wilmington. They'd liquidated the flower shop and cashed in their savings to flip a brick two-bedroom in Hidden Valley.

The valley was definitely hidden. You could fire an aerosoft gun from the pond dead-ending the street and hit the wooden entrance sign announcing the neighborhood.

Jaylin had pocket-knifed her name into the back of that sign. How we met was I found her chiseling mine beside it: *Bailey Elizabeth Cross*, birth certificate style. Said she'd heard my parents chewing me out by it that morning. (I'd just been banished outside, Gameboy confiscated.)

She nodded solemnly to the carving. "You're entrenched in the annals."

I remember thinking she'd mispronounced 'anal' and laughing at a joke she hadn't made.

"Dead-ass," Jaylin pointed the knife at the splintery heap in my yard. "You got designs on those leftovers?"

Yesterday, Mom had found a nest of threadbare pillows in our toolshed and blamed vagrants. That building's demolitioned remnants now rotted in our yard, the first casualty of an aggressive renovation.

My parents had moved on to drywall that morning. They boomboxed James Taylor and swung three-pound hammers in cheerful sync. The move to Wilmington had fused them into one unit. That summer I gagged at their singlemindedness, but I'm old enough now to see how they were confusing forgiveness with agreement.

When Jaylin explained about the fort she was designing, they dropped their hammers and planted their hands on their hips identically.

"I have this mental vision," Jaylin said. "I want to get it in my eyes. Actualize it."

My parents fished their mouths open and shut at each other.

"Just be careful about nails," Mom said.

Jaylin cited her recent tetanus booster.

Dad scavenged us two pairs of garden gloves and told me he was glad to see me doing something.

Jaylin led me into the garage next door. A couch leaked stuffing onto subfloor. A barbell rusted into the uprights of a crooked weight bench. I rubbed the jagged knurling. My dad had Goodwilled his dumbbells before we'd left Raleigh, saying he was done compensating.

"Don't risk tetanus." Jaylin dropped a toolbox into a fat-tired wagon, the kind with wheels designed to tackle heavy sand.

We crammed it full of two-by-fours from the ex-shed. She kept stuffing her face in the crook of her elbow and coughing something.

"What's that?" I asked.

"Asthma. Man the handle," she told me.

I followed her around the retention pond at the end of the street, dragging the wagon over sandy dirt and crabgrass. The brown-black water looked solid. Jaylin said there were mammoth bones on the bottom. When the rainstorms let up in September and the water level dropped, we could wade out and examine them.

I was too busy wheezing to call bullshit. Dragging this wagon was the highest my heart rate had gotten since Gracie Gutierrez pantsed me in my last-ever soccer game. But this was an effort with a comfort. My veins felt snug around my racing blood.

Jaylin led me into a clot of woods behind the pond, cough-muttering intermittently. Narrow pines jutted. Scrub oaks hunched like their trunks had stomachaches.

Fifty yards in, the scrub thinned around a thicker, older tree. Its branches bouqueted out like a firework exploding. White flowers ladened its limbs. The air thickened with this richly musty scent.

"That's not cum." Jaylin petted the trunk. "This is a Bradford. It's a mothersucking invasive species."

Five years later, I'd do something to Wilson Partridge that would fill the camper shell of his Toyota Tundra with an odor like this one. He'd ask why I was crying, what he'd done, and I'd tell him I was thinking of a tree.

Of course, it would really be Jaylin I was thinking of—wondering why an eleven-year-old girl had known the smell of semen.

But that summer I didn't know anything. We leaned eight two-by-fours around the base of the tree. Jaylin climbed into the wagon to nail them to the trunk, but the nails were too short to pass through the planks.

"They look stable enough," I said.

Jaylin's left eyebrow jumped higher than the other. "Ever heard of a hurricane?"

"We're from Raleigh."

"Piedmonter." Her whisper held a grudge, the same way Mom had muttered *vagrants*.

"Most teepees are covered in animal skins," I said, just for something.

"Insensitive." Jaylin made for the retention pond. "You manning the handle or what?"

I wouldn't get my Gameboy back until sunset, and dragging the wagon was fun in a tiring way. I pretended I was a peasant peddling wares.

We hauled out three more loads of planks. Jaylin's cough-muttering grew quieter, but more frequent. Sounded like she was saying *Kim Eyes Up*. Once the fort was done, we fenced off the perimeter with spare planks.

Jaylin nailed a few two-by-fours into crosses and staked them in the sand. "A graveyard for my ambitions," she said, her stare glazing.

I wasn't sure whether she meant for the fort or for me.

I crawled into our insensitive teepee. Jaylin sat with her back against the trunk, reached up, and touched the junction where the two-by-fours met the bark. My fingers fell an inch shy when I tried the same thing.

"It's too short," she said.

"Let's dig out the floor."

Her sigh sounded a decade older than she was. "Tomorrow. I'm out of gumption."

We sat in tired silence, chests-to-knees. Jaylin coughed *Kim Eyes Up* seven times—someone's Twitter handle, I decided. I was looking at the sand-wagon's huge tires, picturing Jaylin inviting me to the beach.

"You surf much?" I asked.

She snorted. "I've never sniffed ocean."

We were twenty minutes away from the Atlantic.

Jaylin turned her mouth into her elbow to cough.

"Kim Eyes Up," I said.

She failed to deem this. "Let's rehydrate."

I manned the wagon through the woods. Turtles bobbed in the retention pond, their shells giving the surface the illusion of boiling. My parents' hammering carried over the water.

"Which one philandered?" Jaylin asked.

I dropped the wagon's handle. "Excuse me?"

"Learn to take a mothersucking joke," Jaylin said. "You want Capris Sun or what?"

I'd've listened to her talk another hour of shit for a sugar rush. I dragged the wagon back onto the street, the back of my mouth going sour with longing.

Jaylin led me past the wagon's garage to the house on the other side of mine. A doorless green Jeep rusted in the driveway. Crystals were superglued to its dashboard. She spanked a taillight with the thoughtless force of compulsion. "Man that wagon around back."

I'd dropped the handle like it was hot. Jaylin picked it up and dragged it around the yard. A brick missing from the back step propped the door. A Thanksgiving smell beckoned me.

"Plea the fifth," Jaylin whispered, then stepped aside to permit me.

Her house's layout matched the one that my parents were ruining. The hall led us past a bathroom and laundry closet and a parallel pair of doors that I guessed led to bedrooms. I socked into a furnitureless, televisionless living room. A nest of pillows and insulated blankets was heaped on the hardwood. Sage burned in abalone shell incense holders. The air was smeary with blue smoke, but all I smelled was casserole.

Jaylin knocked on the kitchen door. "Miss Lady?"

The woman at the sink jumped like Jaylin hadn't announced us and came down with both hands braced on the basin. She was braless under overalls, with sharp shoulder blades just like Jaylin's. Her hair was lumped up in a samurai's bun.

"Kim Eyes Up," Jaylin coughed, but those words sounded wrong.

"Pecan pie." The lady pointed to the fridge, then the oven. "Broccoli casserole's coming."

Jaylin grabbed two Capris Suns and shoved me into the living room.

"That's your mom?"

"Want to trade?" Jaylin was already fleeing down the hall. "Come on."

I followed her out, wondering what I'd just walked into.

The Capris Sun tasted like singing. I sucked it down so fast it started skipping my tastebuds.

Jaylin sipped and swished. "Who's Kim Eyes Up?"

The packed shriveled around my straw. I panted my breath back. "You tell me."

I sort of meant about everything.

My parents' singing trickled over from next door. I was pretty certain only husbands could be philanderers. I said, "You've really never been to the beach?"

Jaylin gave me that grown-up sigh. "Tomorrow. Shovels. Sunrise."

I glanced back at my house—not really mine, but the one my parents were trying to make feel that way. If I went home this early, I'd have a three-pound hammer of my own waiting. "What are you going to do?"

Jaylin tucked my drained Capris Sun under the loose brick. "Ruminate."

My parents were tenting it in the living room. They sent me up a ladder with glow-in-the-dark adhesive stars for the ceiling. The lights worked fine, but we used a battery lamp that night, eating takeout and staring up at my interpretation of constellations. Mom and Dad kept touching each others' non-eating hands. I had a sick hunch that this would be our new homeostasis.

Every restaurant around here seemed to be fusion. That night was—serious—Greek Hibachi. I drenched my gyro in the teriyaki-tzatziki until Mom got afraid it was sugar-laced.

"You've got a friend," she said, confiscating it.

"A mother-something friend," Dad said.

"Mothersucking," Mom said.

They touched hands for six seconds.

I ditched my food and crawled into the tent. My Gameboy sat on my pillow like a diamond. I zipped the tent shut, but could still hear them touching. Miss Lady's shoulder blades simmered behind my eyes like the sun's afterimage. I believed Jaylin had never been to the ocean, even if they did own a Jeep.

Jaylin was waiting at my front door the next morning. She wielded two green folding shovels, the army surplus kind. I didn't hoot which garage she'd raided them from. There were bigger mysteries.

Our fort seemed straighter. I sat with my back against the trunk, reached up and brushed the slanted ceiling. "Do I look taller?"

Jaylin scrunched down her neck. "Only if I do this. Man your shovel."

It's hard to dig from a sitting position. I left the shovel's shaft folded, churning like Miss Lady applying a mixing spoon to gravy. I heaped dirt in front of the fort and tried to push out my shoulder blades.

Jaylin's shovel pinged off of something. "Mothersucker."

I crawled around the tree trunk, hoping she'd struck mammoth tusk, but she was shaking out her hands and staring at a tin lid.

We chiseled it out of the ground with our shovels. A lunchbox-sized case with clasps sealing it.

"Is this yours?" Jaylin asked. "Is it drugs?"

"Don't open it."

She snapped the clasps back and creaked up its lid.

Inside were toppling stacks of photos. The same family grinned in a series of Christmas card poses: a swoopy-haired lady, a tall-bald guy with hips wider than his shoulders, and two boys whose torsos had the same trapezoid shape as his. The boys were fourteen and seven, maybe. They all wore matching knit sweaters and jeans, standing in front of a mossy live oak.

"Do they live here?" I hoped the older boy'd seen me.

Jaylin shook her head. "Trespassers."

"Maybe they were already buried," I said. "The dirt seemed loose yesterday."

"What in suck does that mean?"

We shuffled through the pictures like Yu-Gi-Oh cards. I felt more like the trespasser, but not guilty. Older bro had these James Franco cheekbones. "Guy's cute."

"His hairline's already receding."

That didn't look true.

"Cringe." Jaylin held one up to me. The family stood single-file with their hands on each others' shoulders, faces stacked perfectly: the oldest exactly a head taller than his brother, Mom a head taller than him, Dad tilting his chin into her scalp like he was sniffing.

There were about twenty photos, a dozen or so copies of each. The empty box below was disappointing, but I didn't know what I'd else been hoping for—or even when I'd started hoping.

Jaylin dropped her stack. "I don't give a shit. Keep them."

She hadn't coughed since she'd opened it.

I tucked the pictures into the box. She snapped the lid shut and shoved it out of the fort. We dug until roots started stubbing our shovels. The displaced dirt was heaped halfway up the entrance, barricading us in. It reminded me of the Edgar Allen Poe story where the guy bricks his friend into the basement, only both of us were stuck behind the wall. It was still too shallow in there to stand up.

"I could go for a Capris Sun," I said.

Jaylin crawled out, kicking sandy dirt at me.

I followed and found her hefting the picture box. "You're keeping it?"

She lugged it back to the bank of the retention pond, spun and chucked it with a valiant two-handed toss. The box plunked into the water. Looked less like it was sinking than getting swallowed.

"Insensitive," I said.

She rubbed her hands on my t-shirt. "Those were cursed."

That summer would've gone better if I'd believed her.

We didn't go back to the fort that week. Jaylin was waiting on my doorstep a little earlier every morning, blowing her breaths like she was expecting steam.

Miss Lady's Jeep would already be missing. She maided in Landfall Sundays through Fridays, gone before six and back after eight. I couldn't picture anyone wanting their houses cleaned before sunrise. I couldn't picture Miss Lady doing anything besides baking. Their hardwood was scratched up from sand in the halls. Flour grouted the cracks between their kitchen tiles. The tiles were the little hexagonal ones that you'd expect in a public pool bathroom. I swabbed them with a Brillo pad while Jaylin sipped Capris Sun between trespassings.

By the following Friday, I'd followed her into every garage on that street. We wrote cusses in the dust on car windows and rearranged fridge magnets into our idea of sex positions. Jaylin would swig a can of Coors while I blushed. Neither one of us mentioned the fort or the pictures until a garage door groaned up on us markering smiley faces on the underweared bulges in a stack of *Mandate* magazines.

We bolted out the side door with the homeowner laying on the horn. Jaylin hurdled the flowerbed in the side yard, already four full strides ahead. I chased her down to the dead-end. She'd vanished through the pines before I rounded the retention pond, still squeezing my Sharpie. I ran until I was wheezing the musty scent of the Bradford tree.

Jaylin was already on all fours in the fort, hunching over something. I heard the clasps snap before I ducked in and saw.

The tin box was back, cushioned on a rumpled blanket.

"Told you," she said. "Haunted."

The same photos of that family grinned up at us.

I shuffled through them. Bald dad. Swoopy-haired wife. Son with the cheekbones and totally intact hairline and the younger one, who looked like he hadn't figured out smiling.

"Curses don't get in through your mouth," Jaylin said.

I only realized I'd been holding my breath when she said it. The back of my throat got that pressurized feeling. The photos seemed suddenly radioactive. I dumped them back in the box and slammed the lid, feeling like my fingertips had extra electrons.

"You're sure you don't know them?" Jaylin said.

Now I felt like I did. The blanket the box sat on had crumbs on it. "Someone's living here."

"No shit." Jaylin crawled out with the box. "Come on."

I pressed my nose into the blanket. Smelled like sweet potato pie and spicy incense.

"You gonna roll in it?" Jaylin said.

I followed her back to the pond, trying to figure out how to ask what I wanted her to admit. "We should tell someone."

"And spread the curse?"

"There's no curse."

"Absence of evidence isn't evidence of absence."

It sounded like something Gracie Gutierrez would've said. I hitched up my daisy dukes.

Jaylin shoved the box at me. I backpedaled through the crabgrass.

"That's what I thought." She chucked it into the water with another clumsy shot putter's spin. "We need mothersucking sage."

Back to Jaylin's. The blanket pile in the living room did look smaller. A lighter laid on the hardwood like it had been dropped. I followed a whiff of sweet potatoes to the kitchen.

"She's not in there," Jaylin said.

I peeked into the fridge. Every shelf was loaded with pie trays and casserole dishes. I grabbed a loaf of banana-looking bread from the door-side shelf where my parents would've stored non-canola salad dressing. Miss Lady had cooked enough to feed a dozen, but none of the dishes seemed touched.

"Have it!" Jaylin called.

I peeled off the saran wrap. I was only an hour out from breakfast, but felt like it had been a week. I ate that whole loaf with the fridge open, basking in the square of cool and bright that fell out.

Jaylin coughed words in the living room. Maybe she'd forgotten I was there; maybe she hadn't, and was reminding me. Either way, she spoke slow and loud enough to make out.

Kill myself. That was what she'd been chanting.

I shoved out of the kitchen. She knelt on the blankets, cupping an abalone shell both-handedly—a posture like praying, or offering.

"Why'd you say that?" I asked.

"Takes the pressure off."

The banana bread went cement in my stomach. "Why don't you sleep here?"

Her shoulder blades sharpened through the back of her t-shirt. "Go."

I was still young-dumb enough to listen to what she said instead of her tone.

The hammering had stopped at my house. The front door was locked. I went around back instead of knocking. Al Stewart baritoned through the paint-stained boombox. Something else was rustling, or whispering. I got this sneaky instinct and tiptoed up the hall.

My parents had hammered out all the drywall between the kitchen and living room, islanding the countertop with the stove and dishwasher. 'LOAD BEARING' was Sharpied vertically down a marooned ceiling beam in a capitalized column. A hammer-shaped dent pocked the spot between the 'D' and the 'B'.

For the first time in my life, I realized my parents didn't know what they were doing.

The tent was zipped, the back of it bulging rhythmically. The nylon blistered and drained with a head-shape.

"Kill myself," I whispered—just testing.

The tent stilled.

"What's that?" Dad's voice seemed deeper.

"Nothing."

Zipping and rustling.

"Pete," Mom said, "I locked it."

"Bailey?" Dad called in a pitch back to his.

"You don't need an excuse," Mom said.

I sprinted into the bathroom and locked it.

The next dawn, Jaylin yelled me awake.

I sat up with Dad unzipping the tent. He leaned in from outside. The top half of his sleeping bag hung from his waist like a partially shed snakeskin. I looked from that to the empty space across Mom, who seemed bigger without him spooning her in.

"You slept out there?" I said.

"Bailey Elizabeth Cross!" Jaylin hollered.

"Deal with her," Dad said.

She bounced on our doorstep like a boxer. It was the kind of light that comes right before sunrise, the air brightening like cooking egg whites. She tilted her head like *vamos* and took off for the pond.

If I'd gone inside, she'd've yelled me back out again. I stomped my shoes on and followed her around the retention pond. The pines and oaks seemed farther apart, like the woods had been stretched. Seemed like it took twenty minutes to reach the Bradford tree.

Jaylin pointed to our fort. "Look."

"Nope," I said, but felt like a treadmill was pulling me—like if I didn't walk forward I'd fall off of something. I ducked into the fort.

Another tin box was propped open. The same photos of the same family. Maybe the low light tricked my eyes; maybe I didn't look long enough for the image to stabilize, but I swore they were smirking instead of smiling.

I bolted. Jaylin wrapped me in both arms and tackled me. We smacked the sandy dirt and rolled over flower pedals and pine cones.

I pummeled her with knees and elbows. "Let go!"

She pinned my wrists under her palms and straddled me. "I'm the curse." Her voice more than her weight was what stopped me: her grip had grownup strength, but she spoke with the flat sadness of an adult. A month later, Mom would tell me Dad had gone back to Raleigh in the same monotone.

I slumped limp.

"Ready?" Jaylin said.

I thought she was going to kiss me.

She told me how she'd drowned her sister instead.

Jaylin was four; Maura was two years younger. Maura had torn the best picture out of *Happy as a Tapir*, where the blob-people crawl out of their animal suits. Miss Lady left them soaking in the bathtub to triple-check that she'd pulled the green bean casserole out of the oven. (Jaylin said she remembered what food because she still threw up from the smell of it.) Maura had gone under, and Jaylin had just not let her come up. She held her laced palms out in front of her stomach to show me how she'd put them on the back of Maura's head.

When Miss Lady came back from the kitchen, Jaylin was shaking her sister's shoulders and sobbing.

"The shrink told me I was too young to know better, but how come I was crying?" Jaylin sounded like it was breaking her ribs to talk. She rolled off of me. "I knew what I was doing."

I must've responded, but all I remember is walking out of those woods alone.

Jaylin had to have planted those photos. I couldn't think of any other reason for her to go out to our fort before dawn.

That following fall, I'd start my own nighttime walks. My mom and I were sharing a box-spring in our studio apartment, but I swore I heard echoes when I tossed. So I'd stomp my shoes on and pace laps around the complex, thinking this was how Jaylin must've felt in that furnitureless house. Those had been her pillows my Mom found in the shed. Our fort had been her new nest.

But I was months from such insight that morning. All I wanted to do was crawl down the front of Miss Lady's overalls. I'd've let her call me Maura, but her Jeep was gone. The front door was locked.

A picture was pinned under the loose brick on the back step. I pulled it out.

Jaylin and I hunched under the teepeed two-by-fours of our fort, staring at the picture box. I folded the photo into my pocket.

Jaylin was moping up the street. I ran home before she got to me.

Dad's hammering filled the house, but I didn't see him.

Mom was folding tent poles. She gave me a look like she was choking. "How about the beach?"

The sand squeaked like a bitten animal when you walked on it. Mom dove past the breakers and bobbed for three hours. I squirmed on my towel, feeling myself sunburning, still wearing my daisy dukes with the picture of the fort in the pocket. When she waded back to the beach, I showed it to her.

That ended the renovation. No crime to investigate. No suspect to pursue. Police's sole appeasement was a nightly squad car coasting down our street. Dad hosted open houses while Mom dragged me to the beach. We stayed until the whitewater silvered under the moon, getting home even later than Miss Lady. Her protection felt like a punishment. I couldn't've seen Jaylin if I'd wanted to.

I did try. I was going to tell her about the beach and Dad's hammer, that the curse hadn't stopped me from talking to her. But I'd gotten this smothered feeling walking into her yard. I'd left an index card with our new address under the loose brick on the stoop. Moving was my excuse.

Our house had sold for a loss. Dad moved back to Raleigh and Mom and I moved into a furnished efficiency by UNCW. Our furniture never made it out of the storage unit.

The crystals are missing from Jaylin's Jeep, but the dashboard's corrugated with dried Superglue. A Pizza Hut hat hangs by its snapback from the rearview.

The passenger's seat releases a yeasty, cheesy smell under me. "How's Miss Lady?"

"She stopped driving." Jaylin nods to the wiry hole where the radio should be. "That was her."

She speeds us across town in solid silence, the wind wrongly muted. Night pools like an oil spill beyond the headlights. I put in fingers in the negative space of the radio. The wires feel like they're reaching for me.

We speed past the turn lane for Hidden Valley. First time in five years I've been over here. We'd really only moved up the road, but this neighborhood felt farther away than Dad's condo in Raleigh. I'd been confusing distance with remoteness—a hereditary mistake.

Jaylin brakes into the turn lane in front of the Monkey Junction Exxon, takes a trailer park's first lefthand side-street. Azaleas overflow from shell-studded mulch beds.

She stops two mailboxes shy of the yard with the Bradford tree.

A naval-vessel level of flags jut from the doublewide behind it. The trailer looks moored to its wooden porch. Its windows are lightless.

"It really wasn't you," I say.

She nods to the trailer like, *see*. "I had to keep living there. You got to move."

"I didn't ask to."

"You weren't mad about it, either."

Half a decade she'd stayed in that neighborhood, growing up without knowing who was watching.

Jaylin drops out of the driver's side, leaves the engine rumbling.

"Where you going?"

"We need to establish a sightline."

She folds into this hunching, anime-looking run, arms outstretched behind her. I can picture her cutting class to vape in a dugout, and I'm glad we wound up at different schools. She slams her back against the Bradford and air-traffics her arms at me.

I cram both hands into the dashboard's radio hole. Whoever took our picture could be in that trailer with their nuclear family. Jaylin and I were daughters from homes that had lost isotopes; we should've been the ones eavesdropping. But I'd rather look into other windows.

I crawl behind the wheel and reverse the Jeep.

"Mothersucker!" Jaylin shouts. Light yellows the doublewide's corner window.

I floor it up the road. In the rearview, Jaylin darkens and shrinks.

Two lefts get me back to Hidden Valley. I pull into Jaylin's driveway. Seven cars are parked in the yard of my old house. Four undergraduate types smoke cigars on a porch-length couch, legs fused to one clump under a blanket. Laughter prickles down. Two of the girls up-nod like they know me. I walk past without waving.

A fountain spews in the retention pond. The woods are younger than I remember. A hundred yards back, a sandy clearing opens out of the saplings. Chewed-looking two-by-fours are strewn through the weeds. A charred stump shrivels in the middle. The air's still sour with the Bradford tree's must. I hold its scent's ghost in my lungs.

If I hadn't shown Mom the picture, my parents might've finished renovating. Maybe they'd've worked each other out and I'd've wound up vaping in the dugout with Jaylin. It's not always good to keep trying. I hold my breath until my lungs buck, then release.

Again

Jenny Bates

I walk
slower in
the rain
think slower
breathe slower
then, think
again
thinking being
expressing
breathing being
pressing, some
say magic
is about
breath
a solvent
extraction —
something to
eat, a
union of
sorts, two
halves of
a single
whole
deep, I
suppose
I let
the rain
think for
me, a
job interview
my breath
full of
fire and

flame can't
pass this
test and
slowly
as I
take up
my pen
I know
I won't
apply for
this job
again.

What Changes, What Remains the Same

Karen Bryant Lucas

1970

"Didn't you know what your pastor believed when you hired him? Didn't he preach about it?" the reporter asked.

"Yes," she replied without giving her name, "but we thought that was just *preaching*. We didn't think he was gonna *do* anything about it."

2021

Ridgecrest Baptist Church sits beside NC State Highway 98, its tiny steeple pointing sharply into the sky as if to pin it in place. Next to the two-lane 55-mph road that connects Wake Forest and Durham, it looks exactly as it did in 1969 when my father was pastor there for nine months. Before he was dismissed for practicing what he preached.

In the summer of 2021, I am on my way into Wake Forest on Highway 98. The twists and turns of the road I knew now lie buried deep beneath the waters of Falls Lake, formed in the 1980s when the Neuse River was dammed. The old highway dead-ends into a white metal gate, beyond which is a gravel-covered trail. Here and there, the gray pavement emerges from beneath the gravel, but the yellow and white center lines, almost transparent, lead to where the road disappears beneath the water.

The country road that coiled around old homesteads and farms, has been superseded by a streamlined two-lane highway straight into town, level as far as the eye can see. The farms and fields that I remember have been replaced by housing developments. Clusters of oversized houses with tiny yards have sprung up like mushrooms behind manicured hedges and black iron railings, a reminder that what was a cozy seminary town of 4,000 when we lived here, is now home to 55,000 people. A lot has changed.

But Ridgecrest Baptist Church looks exactly the same as it did more than fifty years ago.

I drive past the church and turn left onto Stony Hill Road, looking for a modest red brick ranch-style house that no longer exists, but that nevertheless still stands at an intersection in my memory between innocence and experience. The carefully curated innocence of Whiteness. The bitter experience of racist violence.

That house was the parsonage of Ridgecrest Baptist Church and, for two months in 1969, my family's home. Its absence haunts the shoulder of Stony Hill Road.

1969

I was 15 going on 16 when my father, a student at the seminary in Wake Forest, was installed as the pastor of Ridgecrest. About six miles west of town, the church, having split from another well-established church about seven years before, was struggling. Under my dad's leadership, attendance went up, offerings increased. The church was so pleased that they pulled out the plans for a new parsonage, previously shelved for lack of funds, and began building it that summer.

They surprised my parents by installing a heat pump to regulate automatically the temperature in the house, at extra cost. In the family room, they included a fireplace. And custom-made wood paneling.

"It can't be matched," they said. "If the paneling gets damaged, the whole thing will have to be ripped out and replaced."

They were extremely proud of that paneling.

By September, the house was finished, and we moved in.

A month later, my mother pulled me into the kitchen. It was late afternoon, I was just home from school. The days were getting shorter, and the sun was already moving behind the trees. She sat me down at the table to talk to me about a party I was planning.

"Some people are going to be upset," she said, "that you are inviting Bettie and Jean, William, Mike and Silas, and Marjorie." The names of some of my Black friends.

"Are you sure you want to invite them?"

Every year since I'd entered high school, I had thrown a party for my friends. Anywhere from 10 to 15 of them would show up. Usually the party was planned for the fall, when we could still get outside and play badminton or volleyball. We would set up nets in the wide yard next to the small seminary duplex where we lived before. Dad grilled hot dogs and hamburgers, and Mom spread a long table with condiments and buns, paper plates and plastic utensils.

Of course, since the Wake County school system was still largely segregated even as late as 1968, all of my friends were White.

That changed in the fall of 1969, the beginning of my junior year. About nine Black students, also juniors, elected to transfer from the all-Black W.E.B. DuBois School to the predominantly White Wake Forest High School.

For a number of years, my Christian parents had been teaching me and my brothers that, as the children of one God, we were all siblings—"brothers and sisters," as they said—regardless of our race or color. That we were equal in the eyes of God. Equally beloved of God. Both of them were born in southeastern Virginia and raised in the Jim Crow South of the 1930s and 40s, but they found it impossible to ignore the civil rights movement, and particularly the powerful preaching and example of Martin Luther King, Jr.

Slowly, and not easily, they had come to believe that segregation was morally wrong. And that's what they taught us.

I found it easy to make friends among the Black students. I wanted them to feel welcomed, and, since we were all juniors, we were in many of the same classes. We were just beginning to get to know each other when I decided to throw another party, this one in the much larger family room of the parsonage. Naturally my new friends were on the guest list.

Now my mother sat across the table from me, asking me if I was sure I wanted to include them.

"Mom!" I said, "If I can't have a party with all my friends, I don't want to have a party at all!"

"Yes, that's what your father and I thought you would say, and we agree with you. We just want it to be your decision."

I knew, even as an idealistic and innocent 16-year-old, that many White people, including church members and some of our friends, disapproved of our hosting an interracial party. One by one, my White friends told me they weren't coming. Stopping me in the hallway between classes, hit and run: "I'm so sorry, but I'm not going to be able to come to your party after all. We're going out-of-town that weekend." "I have to go Christmas shopping with my aunt." "Our relatives are coming to visit that weekend, and I need to be at home." The list of excuses was wide, but shallow. The real reason lay clearly visible at bottom: they refused to attend a party where there would be what they called "mixin'."

Some of my Black friends also decided not to come. For notably different reasons. The father of one said to her, "An integrated party? *In the Harricans?*" End of discussion.

The Harricans (pronounced *HAIR*-k'ns) was an area of indeterminate latitude and longitude. As one Wake County sheriff famously said, if you ask where the Harricans is, the answer is always "a few miles up the road." It got its name after a hurricane devastated the hardscrabble farming community trying to eke a living out of ungracious soil. Many folks gave up on farming and turned to the manufacture of moonshine. White lightnin', corn licker. In a dry county, like Wake County at the time, the Harricans' claim to fame was that you could always be sure to find a Mason jar of something from a still out in the woods that would take the edge off your pain and the lining off your innards.

When my father accepted the call to pastor Ridgecrest Baptist Church early in 1969, he was not naive. Most, if not all, of the people who lived in the tight-knit community were White, the descendants of Confederate soldiers, and proud of it. Some of them gave their children the names of Confederate generals, like Nathan Bedford Forrest. Or Stonewall, for Stonewall Jackson.

And they were dyed-in-the-wool segregationists. He heard tell of one person who had said that, if his daughter were to date a "n****r," he would "shoot them both down in the road like dogs." And there was another church right up the road from the parsonage, established 20 years after the end of the Civil War, whose constitution clearly stated that "if a n****r steps foot on our property, we will throw him off."

The week before the party, the deacons of Ridgecrest called a special meeting. Only one item was on the agenda: to convince the pastor to cancel his children's "integrated" party.

"If you allow this party to go on," they said, "we will ask for your resignation."

My father argued that he was not trying to force the church to integrate, and that we were not insisting that church members plan interracial parties in their homes.

"I have been teaching my children to judge people on the content of their character, not on the color of their skin," he said. "How can I tell them now that their friends are not welcome in our home because they are Black?"

But as news of the party circulated, the anger roiling in the White community began to alarm the deacons. These were people they had known and lived beside for years, decades. They were afraid that the church would lose respect and influence among their White neighbors.

And they were anxious about possible damage to the brand-new parsonage. At least one mentioned the custom wood paneling. "It can't be matched," he reminded my father.

The discussion went round and round for two, three, four hours.

Finally, one of them piped up, "Well! If you allow this party to go on as planned, one thing's for sure: we will ask for your resignation."

"Well, I'm gonna have to do what I have to do," my father said, "and I guess y'all are just gonna have to do what you have to do."

The meeting ended in a stalemate. At least two of the deacons reportedly went door-to-door in the Harricans over the next few days, fanning the flames of outrage.

2021

I am staying with old friends, White friends in Wake Forest. When I tell them I'm writing a book about what happened to my family, and to the town, in the late 60s, their response is less than encouraging. "This place has changed so much since you lived here." "It's not the same town anymore, so many new people have moved in." They inform me that Wake Forest has become less a separate town and more a bedroom community for people who work in the Research Triangle, in Raleigh, Durham, and Chapel Hill.

"No one remembers what happened that long ago."

While I am in town, one of my Black classmates from back in the day invites me to a cookout at her house. Everyone there is Black, except for me and one other White friend.

After eating ourselves silly, we gather in the family room and plop down into comfy chairs. The mother of one of my Black former classmates points at me and says, "Oh! Is this the girl that had that party?" Everyone nods.

"Do people still remember the party?" I ask.

"Oh, yes," a Black friend answers, "they remember. They act like they don't, but they remember."

1969

The day of the party, December 13, a Saturday, was a brilliantly sunny, crisp day. Brown bermuda grass, covered in frost, crackled underfoot in the cold. Every exhale hung in front of my face in a small cloud. The kind of weather that says that the holidays are just around the corner. Cold enough to build a fire in the fireplace!

At midday I returned home from a Beta Club convention to find my father out in the yard doing target practice.

"This old shotgun Dad gave me when I was 14," he said. "Just want to make sure it will still shoot."

Inside the parsonage, my mother was moving the lamps in the living room over to the picture window on the front of the house and closing the curtains.

"Mom, what are you doing?"

"Oh," she answered lightly, "I'm just moving the lamps over to the curtain."

"Yeah…. But why?"

"Well, so that, if anyone walks through the living room tonight, their shadow won't be cast on the curtain." Her voice was higher than usual. "You know, in case there's any trouble…."

"Do you think there's gonna be trouble!"

"No, no…." Her voice trailed off. "But just in case."

In the early evening Dad and I drove into town to pick up two of my friends, one White and one Black. It was already dark. At the Stony Hill Fire Department, just down the road from us, a large sign announced, "TURKEY SHOOT December 13!" The parking lot out front was full, and behind the station, a large yard was flooded with lights.

On the way back, as we passed, my White friend rolled down the window and, as a joke, called out, "Hey! We're having an integrated party! Come on down—"

"ROLL UP THAT WINDOW!" my dad snapped. Without another word she rolled it up, and we turned into the driveway in uneasy silence.

As the party began, I was on edge. My grandparents, visiting over the weekend, were entertaining my 9-year-old brother, watching TV in my parents' bedroom. My friends and I, along with my 14-year-old brother, were all gathered in the family room, directly behind the living room. Music was playing on the stereo. The Christmas tree lights sparkled. There was a hearty fire crackling in the fireplace.

An hour passed. I began to relax.

At about 9 pm, my youngest brother came padding through the family room in his pajamas on the way to the kitchen. He wanted popcorn.

Popcorn sounded like a good idea to us teenagers, too. We all crowded toward the kitchen. Which, in hindsight, was lucky, because moving toward the kitchen moved all of us away from the center of the room.

I was standing by the kitchen door, waiting to go in, a Black friend to my right and a White friend just in front of me.

The Fifth Dimension was singing, "This is the dawning of the Age of Aquarius, Age of Aquarius…."

BOOM. Behind me I heard an explosion, sharp and sudden like a thunderclap. I spun around to see the wood paneling splintering, pockmarked with holes. *Oh no,* I thought, *Mom is gonna be so mad*. I couldn't make sense out of what I saw. Maybe someone had lit a firecracker and thrown it behind the couch—

Just then my father shouted, "Hit the floor! And cut the lights!"

We stood there for a moment, stunned.

"HIT THE FLOOR!" he yelled. We dropped where we stood.

He ran to the bedroom to retrieve and load his shotgun. To my mother he said, "Call the police." Then he ran out onto the carport.

The gunman was already gone, but his livid message was sprayed across the living room wall. Seventeen pellets of double-aught buckshot, the kind used for hunting large game, crashed through the picture window and struck the white wall, seven of them with enough force to plunge through it and into the family room. One pellet even embedded itself in the stone of the fireplace.

And, around each black hole in the family room, the custom wood paneling splayed out, shredded.

While we waited for the sheriff to arrive, my mother plopped down on the hearth. "Well," she said bitterly, "at least we didn't get blood on their precious parsonage."

2022

I sort through the newspaper articles and other materials from Wake Forest that my mother carefully collected in a large storage bin. At the bottom I come across a small plastic box. It rattles.

Inside are all of the spent shotgun pellets that Mom painstakingly gathered from the walls and floor of the parsonage. Each pellet, about the diameter of the pencil I am using to write this story, is flattened into a rounded piece of gun-metal gray, with a jagged fissure across one side.

I dump them into my hand. They are small, but remarkably heavy.

1969

45 minutes. That's how long we crouched on the linoleum floor, waiting for the deputy sheriff to cross the six miles between town and the parsonage. The first words out of his mouth were, "Well, it's kinda hard to catch 'em 'less ya catch 'em red-handed." He took one of the pellets of buckshot and slipped it into his pocket.

The next morning was Sunday. At church, the deacons followed my father into the pastor's study and closed the door.

"We want you to resign," they said.

"I'm not going to resign," he answered. "If you want to get rid of me, you'll have to go on record."

"Well, we don't want you to preach."

"Well," Dad said, "you have a problem. Because your constitution says that you can't call a special business meeting until after the worship service. Which means that until then, I am still your pastor. And as long as I am pastor, that is my pulpit, and I *will* preach. You don't have to come hear it. But I'm *gonna* preach."

At the business meeting after the service, the vote was 27 in favor of firing my dad, 11 against, and 20 abstentions.

They told us they wanted us out of the parsonage as soon as possible.

On Monday afternoon, as we were moving the last of our things, reporters drove up. They apologized. "We only just found out about the shooting." Later we learned that the police report had been "filed in the wrong box," where it remained undiscovered for four days.

Dad took them through the house. He stood for a photo pointing to the holes where the shot came through the window.

Then they asked me for a photo.

I remember, as in a dream, stepping carefully through the broken glass. The photographer wanted a shot of my profile against the jagged edges of what remained of the picture window. He snapped several photos in rapid succession. In the one chosen for that first article, my eyes are stunned, unfocused. I am looking toward but not directly at the living room wall scarred by small black holes. In fact, I don't remember ever looking closely at that wall. I wish I had, but maybe it's just as well I didn't.

Now I look searchingly at the photo, but it is no use. I am so far removed from the naive 16-year-old girl I was. The shotgun blast severed my past from my future. Any innocence I formerly possessed lay shattered across the living room floor as surely as the glass of a picture window that showed me only what Whiteness wanted me to see.

2024

When our first Black president was elected in 2008, I immediately called my father. "I never thought I would live to see this day," he said. We wept. For both of us, it was vindication for a lifetime spent practicing what he preached and the sacrifices our family made, beginning with Wake Forest.

It was easy in that moment to imagine that the story I have to tell was a relic of the past, no longer relevant.

I wish. I wish it were that simple to uproot racism and White supremacy.

In 2020, I watched in horror the video of a young Black man being gunned down—lynched, in effect—while jogging through a White neighborhood. Likewise the footage, captured by a teenage girl, of a Black man being pinned to the ground under a White police officer's knee until the life had been squeezed out of him.

I knew I needed to tell the story. Not the way I would have told it in the past, but with awareness about the way Whiteness manifests in me. I need to tell it and, at the same time, investigate my own Whiteness.

"Just preaching," the anonymous woman said.

Like preaching, writing is words. But words can be action, if they interrogate the past. If they reveal what has been hidden or erased, pushed aside or willfully forgotten. Words are action, if a lived life stands behind them or inhabits them. Like the house that bore silent witness to a story many would like, perhaps, to forget.

I begin with NC Highway 98. A road I used to know, but that I no longer recognize. Partly because the road has changed, and partly because I am no longer the same.

I begin with a church frozen in time, and a house whose absence haunts me. I begin with the telling of this story.

The Caretaker

Rick Forbess

Chloe sits on the rectory basement floor weeping to a Celine Dion song, not noticing the choir director's daughter standing half way down the stairs. She must have been there for a while, because when Chloe turns, she sees the girl crying too. Chloe fumbles to hide the open bottle of vodka, but too late. Another calamity. Repeating worn out sermons for weeks, side swiping cars in the church parking lot, wearing a blouse with an unnoticed sauce stain, and now this.

The girl mouths, "I'm sorry."

"No worries," is the best Chloe could do, and that in a faked cheerfulness.

The girl walks back up and closes the door without speaking. Chloe gathers herself and follows within a few seconds. She wobbles at the top of the stairs, but makes it to the sofa facing the backyard bird feeders.

How did it all go so wrong? She recalls the camping trip in the wilderness of northern Maine. Dropping acid with a group of friends. The giant white oak revealing an indifferent universe. Restoring belief in a loving God and his power to end her drinking problem through hours of prayer. But it had not come to pass.

On a December night two weeks after "the basement incident", Chloe is fired by a group of kind Unitarian Universalists who were friends and supporters. The board's counseling and warnings over the last eighteen months had flopped, but they decide unanimously to hold off on the termination date and public announcement until after Christmas.

The chairperson asks for a few moments with Chloe alone.

"Chloe, this is very hard for all of us, but I want you to please let me know if I can help out in any way. Promise to contact me at any time if you need some support. Will you promise?"

"Yes, but I'll be okay," she lies, "Alesandro and I will move on with our lives."

Chloe believes her life in the ministry is over and that this third firing will break Alesandro's heart. During her first year of seminary, she joined AA and attended sporadically until meeting Alesandro, the model member. She fell in love with his rational way of making sense of the world, his genuine kindness, and his sense of humor. When she proposed on their second date, he laughed and kidded her for taking so long to ask.

Alesandro takes the bad news better than she believed and convinces her that a trip to the Bahamas will restore her confidence and pride, but it does not, so after only two days on the island she musters her courage. She stands on the deserted beach at dusk staring out to the dim line separating water from sky. Traces of her footsteps zig zag past an old skiff with all but its partially exposed ribs buried in the sand and beyond that to a point where the shore curves and disappears a quarter of a mile away. She removes her straw hat and lets it fall to her side. For several seconds she stands with her eyes fixed on the darkening horizon before bending for the hat and then slinging it frisbee-style toward the sea. It falls short, but her second try hits the mark, and she watches the hat ride the waves onto the shore and out again several times. When it finally sinks in the retreating surf, she glances back to a wooden stairway rising to a cottage perched high on a sandy cliff. After a few seconds she exhales, turns, and walks into the Atlantic wearing her summer dress.

Owing to the seabed's gentle slope, she's only waist deep seventy-five yards from shore, but trudges along, stumbling occasionally, until stepping into a forty-feet deep, reef-encircled pool and plunging without warning. She goes limps and begins a descent that picks up speed faster than expected. When she opens her eyes, dark coral walls, indistinct and imposing in the failing light, surrounded her. At the count of three she inhales deeply, but she panics when something brushes her right calf.

With two strokes, she resurfaces and circles in place to face inland. Right away she begins to cough and then vomits salt water and booze through her mouth and nose. Waves push her inland a few feet, and when she manages to touch the sandy bottom with her toes, she alternates walking and dog paddling until reaching the beach where she lies on her stomach, waves lapping around her ankles. She rolls to her back and pushes up to sit for a moment listening to the waves' steady cadence. What will Alesandro think if he sees me like this?

Chloe stands and walks to the stairway for the labored climb back to the cottage. The sunflower patterns of the dress cling to her small frame like a second skin, but she knows there is no allure. Those days are long past. She arrives wet, hatless, and sharply aware that she is incapable of drowning herself.

The screen door slaps closed behind her, and Molly's startled bark pierces the quiet. Alesandro glances up from the book he's reading, but before he says anything, she does.

"Son of a bitch. I slipped. Waded in too far and lost my balance."

"You slipped? God, you're soaked. Are you okay? ."

He doesn't press for more. Her lie protects them both.

After a warm shower and changing into a nightgown, she joins Alesandro in the small kitchen where he's making tea and boiling eggs. He pulls out a chair for her at the wooden table and kisses her on the cheek. Insects drawn to the track lighting's soft glow bounce off the window screens. He serves the eggs cut in half and tea with a spoonful of honey like she prefers and then sits across from her holding his cup in both hands. Molly lies next to Chloe's chair, glancing up occasionally.

"Remember the A-frame we stayed in on our honeymoon, Chloe?"

"Of course, why would you ask?"

The reply has an edge to it that surprises her.

"This place reminds me of it. It has the same intimacy - open concept, cozy."

"I hadn't thought of it that way."

Chloe stares into her empty tea cup. She glances around at the two-burner gas range, wicker couch and chairs in the living area, antique looking floor lamps, and landscape prints on the walls. Even the short ladder to the loft bedroom is similar, but thirty-five years ago the climb was easier, and the view out the window was of the Rockies rather than the Atlantic. She remembers two pictures from then – Alesandro sitting in a chair he'd pulled out to the small deck and her feeding a carrot to a donkey that wandered up, and she remembers the patches of wildflowers and snow on the hikes above tree line, and the thunderstorm during the ride on the narrow gauge train to the old mining town, and the souvenir mugs from the gift shop in Santa Fe, and her disappointment that the sex didn't seem magical.

Alesandro lowers his plate and pats Molly's head while she licks the crumbs. "I think we're blessed to have this place to ourselves for the week, and you get to be alone with a community college math teacher, presently retired."

"Very funny, Alesandro. Blessed? Really? By whom? Our lord in heaven? "

Alesandro exaggerates a sigh. "Oh, come on, Chloe. It's just a figure of speech. Lucky. Fortunate. We've been fortunate."

"I'm fortunate to have you, but I've made an awful mess of everything."

When Alesandro reaches across the table, Chloe pulls her hands away to cover her face and sobs.

"Chloe, it's okay. That's behind us. Tomorrow's our last day here. Let's start over."

"I'm tired of screwing up, Alesandro. It's easy for you. You've been sober for decades. I hold on for a couple of years if that. Pathetic."

"That doesn't matter so much. I look at you and I think about how much I love the person you are, your strength and goodness. You've always fought for every disadvantaged person or group you came across. That's what I think about, not the slip ups."

"I'm a hypocrite, Alesandro, a fraud. I'm an ordained minister who doesn't believe in God, and I'm a drunk who was booted out of her church."

"Please don't talk that way, Chloe. It hurts when you say these things. Please don't."

Alesandro's knee crackles when he stands, and Chloe stumbles forward but braces herself with both arms on the table top when she pushes her chair back and tries to get to her feet.

"Vertigo," she says at the same moment he says, "Arthritis", and they both chuckle.

When he finishes tidying up the kitchen, Alesandro joins Chloe in bed, the glow of two Kindles illuminating their faces. She pulls back the sheets and thin bedspread to cool in the humid warmth of the night. Alesandro reaches to pat her thigh, and his reassuring touch is welcomed.

"This is my favorite part of every day," she says.

He falls asleep first, as usual, and Chloe lies on her back in the dark counting the seconds between the crashing waves. The game she plays with herself is to think of as many things to live for as she can during the six second intervals.

She slips from bed, careful not to wake Alesandro. Molly follows her to the front porch and then to the deck attached to the stairs leading down to the beach. Chloe steps off the deck and reaches under a clump of yellow elder bushes to find a half-full bottle of vodka. She takes two long draws, pours the bottle empty, and tosses it toward the beach. For several seconds she stands with arms crossed, watching cloud shadows cast by the moon race across the bay until Molly's whine signals that it's time to go inside.

When she slips into bed and snuggles close to Alesandro, he whispers, "You came back."

"I always do," she says.

When Chloe wakes, a dream's blurred images and an unsettling feeling she can't name linger and then fade, leaving her with a sense of something familiar but impossible to pin down. A trace of a memory fades quickly when she directs her attention to it, and she's left with the facts of the matter. Life is a process that begins and ends, has whatever meaning one gives it, and is all we have. Her marriage to Alesandro and Molly's unjudging loyalty may be enough.

The week they return from vacation, Alesandro learns from a fellow AA member that the hospice service he works for needs a part time chaplain. "Someone who doesn't push the Bible talk, but can bring it if a person wants it."

"This is perfect for you, Chloe."

"Perfect? Really? Have you forgotten how my last job ended?"

"No, of course not, but these people need someone like you. They need comforting."

Tending to the spiritual needs of people in their dying days so soon after the alcohol-fueled saunter into the ocean seems perverse, but Alesandro convinces her to accept her more noble self.

As it turns out, hospice work is a great fit for Chloe. She benefits as much, or perhaps more, than the patients. "This is wisdom," she often tells herself in the presence of a dying person's honesty and genuineness. Most say it's all about love – regrets about holding back, gratefulness for that received, grasping for what remains.

Some of what she hears is hard to buy into but comforting nonetheless. Last week a man in his 80's talked about the certainty of reuniting with every dog he's ever had, and that notion leaves Chloe wistful for Molly and encouraged about whatever lies ahead.

On this morning gold finches and cedar waxwings share the feeders with warblers and blue jays, and the early morning sun glistens on leaves wet from the storm that passed through not long before dawn. Chloe dresses, has a cup of coffee, and then raises the bed to give Alesandro a better view of the blooming Rhododendrons. She pulls the covers back and lies on her side next to him, fully clothed.

She has joined him this way often since the bed was moved into the living room, so when the nurse arrives to begin her shift, it will seem normal. He lays his arm across her chest, a sign that he knows she's there. Glancing around the familiar room, she lingers on the picture of the two of them standing on the porch of the island bungalow. His arm is draped over her shoulder, and hers is around his waist. Molly is looking up at her. Alesandro is leaning on her.

Sleeping on the Job

Richard Allen Taylor

After "A Naiad," oil on canvas
by John William Waterhouse, 1893

The spirit girl stands in the edge of the stream, naked,
nubile, completely if not perfectly female, fresh-faced,

dark hair spilling over her shoulders. Saplings grow
along the bank, and she leans into them, grasping

a single slender tree in each hand as if she were a real girl
gripping the bars of a cage, looking from outside in, watching

a sleeping animal. The object of her gaze is Hylas, young
companion of Hercules. He sleeps, also naked, except

for an animal skin—leopard perhaps, or cheetah—covering
his loins. But he's just a boy, really, perhaps her age,

which is timeless for a naiad, a water nymph who watches over
the stream, unless the flow she guards weakens or stops.

Only then will she grow old. Were it not for the ancient Greeks,
we might equate this pair with Adam and Eve, this scene

with the Garden of Eden. But it's not a garden. It's a wild,
mystical place with meandering stream and muddy red banks

curving around a grassy lea fading from green to brown
in late summer. It must be summer, as neither Hylas

nor the naiad seems to suffer from the lack of clothes.
Sparse vegetation surrounds the boy, who lies half-turned

toward the artist, one leg tucked under the other, head nestled against the base of a tree slightly thicker than a baseball bat,

a reference that would mean nothing to Hylas or the naiad,
but might be familiar to the artist, since baseball was invented

decades before this picture was painted. Hylas' commander,
Hercules, would not have cared about baseball, though he might

have appreciated the masculine symbolism of the bat. He sent
Hylas to search for fresh water, not to take a nap. So I'm worried

about Hylas, not just that he and the naiad are naked
in the wilderness, not just that people in later centuries will debate

whether this picture is pornography or art. (I know art when I see it).
What worries me is that Hylas has put himself in danger here

and doesn't know it. Feeling the need to intervene, I tap the artist
on the shoulder and ask him to take a break while I wake the boy

and try to talk some sense into him. I tell him, look, you need to fill
your water bag and get back to Hercules ASAP. He needs fresh water

for the crew and you shouldn't be hanging around nymphs like
this one. I gesture to my left, toward the naked girl.

What nymph? he asks. I look around.

I guess she left with the painter, I tell him. But nymphs can be
dangerous, you know. In 1896, if you're not careful, you'll be

trapped in a different painting titled "Hylas and the Nymphs"
and you'll go down in mythology as a foolish young man who

allowed himself to be seduced by seven ravishingly beautiful
naiads before disappearing forever.

So, he replies, what are my options?

42 *Richard Allen Taylor*

Glass Stars

Vera Guertler

On a mid June afternoon my two daughters and I arrive with damp necks and sweat trickling through our clothes after our two and a half hour drive southward. With the Engine light appearing on the dashboard midway up our mountainous climb, we chose to open our windows for the last hour of our trip to Zacharelli's Gardens. Between the seats lay the wedding invitation of my former husband's niece Rebecca. She selected this sylvan site brimming with wildflowers and mosquitos circling a small pond. As we leave our vehicle, we see rows of white plastic chairs saturated by the sun. The grass muffles the sound of heels but not of polyester suits, chiffon, and taffeta squeezing into the narrow rows. Once seated, some of us slip pinched toes out from shoes grown tight by the pitch of 3 o'clock.

Rebecca and Lloyd exchange their vows next to two stone angels dribbling water. Behind us, I hear my former husband's name and turn to see him lower himself into his seat. My daughters and I recognize only his family members amidst unfamiliar faces that fan out in repeating semi-circular rows. Once newly declared husband and wife stroll past us, voices and waists rise around us. Some of my daughters' cousins signal them to come to their side. Meanwhile, I move toward the large reception tent where ice cascades into glasses aswirl with pink moscato and lemonade. A few guests bump tightly arranged tables of hors d'oeuvres and brush my backside along the way. I decide to walk out of the tent toward the rim of pines beside the parking lot and wait til the spaces between tables thin some. On the edge of the lot, my former husband leans against the trunk of his Chevy. Even from a distance, I see his thinned hair that I had recently glimpsed at his hospital bedside when my daughters and I were called by nurses to tell us of his near fatal heart attack. While standing in the hallway with his Cardiologist, our daughters had asked her what they could do to help their father. The doctor tilted her head towards the curtained bed and murmured, "Well, if you can convince him to stop smoking that would be the most likely thing to improve his chances of survival going forward."

Now he spots me across the parking lot and gives a nod, as he folds one arm across his chest, while the other hand holds a cigarette. Just at that moment, our daughters arrive at my side and one begins with "Mama, why are you out here–" Then both turn to look in his direction and see his pursed lips. They bend their heads down and walk away without saying another word.

Later, when he takes his place at Table 6, he raises his glass to his face as I pass by. At Table 7, the girls and I perch our hands upon white linen, while waiting to be called to the buffet line. Over lemony chicken sprinkled with crabmeat, we answer the questions of our tablemates about our work and schooling. I bend to pick up my napkin and then half turn to glance at my former husband. Beneath the star shaped lights, he offers a thin-lipped smile. Even under bright strings of stars, his tallow colored face bears the look of a candle no longer lit.

As waitstaff round the tables, pouring more drinks, the band finishes warming up and starts to play. The lead vocalist invites the bride and groom to their first dance. Soon thereafter, the singer instructs the father of the bride to lead his daughter, Rebecca, to the dance floor, and the groom his mother. I suddenly remember years ago dancing in my wedding dress with my uncle, as my husband's mother tightly embraced her son under a spotlight. I'd heard her whisper that he could always come home anytime if he wanted. She'd worn pale pink chiffon that later bore tears and gravy.

After their dance, the music begins to play louder. I look over to Table 7 and find the seat of the man who once was my husband empty. He must've slipped through the crowd like a knot suddenly loosened, and chose to drive away through the dark wet woods. It was in woods like these, full of whispers and sweat, that we first met many Junes ago.

Now I stay to dance under the glass stars of the wedding tent. The raying lights illuminate my daughter's eyes before she turns to sway along with her sister. The singer croons, "take me to the moon…" and I imagine someone I once knew flying down Highway 81. Fast becoming another blur under a starless sky.

Strangers on a Train

Emily Wilson

I notice the boy in the seat across the aisle. Slyly, I watch him. It's easy since we are facing each other. A book is perched on his knee, a small one with yellow pages. The other knee is bouncing in tandem with the train car rattling against the track. His hair is messy and dark, curling at the nape. Long limbs clothed in black. He has a careless appearance in the way only the beautiful can have. The rest of us have to try harder.

I have a knowing sense he's American and studying abroad. We have a knack for recognizing each other. We all have the same habit of triple checking train tickets. The same reebok sneakers and baggy over-shirts: the college uniform. American students have an unspoken alliance, always giving each other smiles and looks of acknowledgment. Sometimes we ask each other where we live, where we go to school, what places we've visited. Then we share tips about the tube in London, the overnight bus to Dublin, the sangria in Lisbon. We warn of pickpockets and offer to take each other's picture. I find these alliances exciting in a camaraderie sort of way, leaving my cheeks flushed and eyes glassy. There's an intensity about their singularity. Speaking to someone you will never see again. The freedom to be outgoing and say stupid things. Sheer thrill.

The boy leaves. I wonder where he's gone. He returns with a dark foamy drink. An Americano. I wanted to order a latte but now I can't-too amateurish. He takes a sip, the foam sticking to his top lip. He licks the froth away. Suddenly, I'm staring into his eyes. They are brown with flecks of gold. I peer down at the book in my lap, my pulse quickening. I feel his attention on me. My chin begins to feel damp. I don't look at him again. *So much for being bold.*

The ticket taker walks through the cabin, rifling through tickets and passports. When I hand over mine, the man asks a string of questions, investigating whether or not I have a bomb in my suitcase. Then he checks the boy's passport across the aisle, asking the same questions. The boy's answers are identical to mine. The ticket taker moves on. My eyes do not. And I'm shocked to find the boy staring back at me.

Here it is: the shared acknowledgment.

"Where are you studying?" he asks.

"Paris," I say, pretending he didn't catch me stare down the foam on his lip.

"I haven't made it there yet," he says.

"But you will?"

He shrugs. "It's likely, isn't it? I go somewhere every weekend."

"How do you decide where you're going?"

"Just pick the cheapest train ticket."

I smile. "Sounds about right."

"And yourself?" he asks.

"Cheapest hostel I think is decent."

He grins. "Decency is an important factor, isn't it?"

"My wallet was almost stolen in one in Milan."

"My bed in Barcelona had pubes on the pillowcase."

I cover my mouth. "I'm gagging."

"Me too."

We discuss where we are from, the colleges we attend and subjects we're studying. If we have any connection to each other's cities or schools we list those too. Ours are only very loose. He asks if I like traveling alone. I tell him I prefer to be alone most of the time, traveling or not.

"That sounds like the characteristic of a sociopath," he says.

"But a sociopath would never admit that," I say.

"Well, you would know."

Surprising myself, I laugh.

He looks at me, waiting.

I shrug. "Americans have an obsession with European partying. I'm not sure I understand the craze. You can get drunk at home. Why do they need to cross an ocean to be unconscious in foreign night clubs?"

"So you needed a break from the drunkards."

"I did."

"Are you very moral then?" He smirks. "A good little school girl."

I fold my arms over my chest like a barrier. "I hate when people do that. Patronize someone for caring."

"That's not what I'm doing."

"You are. There's nothing wrong with caring about my experience abroad, wanting more than partying. Who knows when I'll have the opportunity again?"

For some reason he laughs then, noticing my expression, stops. "I don't disagree."

"Then why are you?"

"I'm only teasing."

I shift in my seat. "Alright."

"Flirting actually."

"Oh."

"Yeah." He smiles. "Seems like I'm not doing the best job."

"No." I wipe the corner of my eye. "I'm just hard to flirt with I think."

"I can see that."

I make a face at him. "You're still not doing well."

"Right." He tilts his head. "Has anyone ever told you you're a bit intimidating?"

"Only those who are intimidated."

"Is that a lot of people?"

"Like I said. I prefer to be alone."

His brows crease. "Do you wish I would leave you alone? It's a bit confusing since you keep watching me drink my coffee."

"Sorry, what?" I shift my ear toward him. "I can't hear you over the sound of your ego."

He smiles. "I'm Leonard."

"You've named your ego? How cute."

"No. My ego's name is Non-existent."

"Ingrid," I blurt.

"Is your ego name?"

"Sure."

We play cards. Leonard buys me coffee from the dining cart. I give in and order a latte.

"I'll pay you back," I say.

"No need."

"I will."

"No need"

"I still will."

He rolls his eyes. "My god."

He's going to Brussels. I'm going to Amsterdam. He's excited for waffles. I'm excited for pancakes. There's a stillness about him that makes words flow from my mouth like water. I find myself telling him way too much, like my sister's miscarriage. How it felt like a death was happening inside my body too, but I couldn't say that to her. It would've seemed insensitive. He says it wasn't, that he understands. He tells me about loneliness, how it's emerged throughout the semester, especially when it's cold outside. I tell him it has for me too. We talk about the adventure of it all, being so far from home, how satisfying and independent we feel. We talk about our insignificance as campus life continues without us back home, not missing us at all. I feel a sense of lightness as we converse, my skin tingling. I feel happy. Important. He'll be getting off in an hour. I know I'll be sad when he leaves, disappearing into the abyss of life, never to be found again.

He misses his parents, doesn't miss his brother. He has a tattoo of twin stars on the side of his index finger. I asked what it meant. He said he and his brother got them when he was a teenager. So now I'm desperate to know what happened, why he no longer misses his brother.

I've been reading a book about grief. It's sitting on the foldout table between our seats, unopened. He squints to read the title.

"I find intense emotions fascinating," I say as a way of explaining.

"Why?"

I rub the front cover with my thumb. "I'm unsure if mine are normal or not."

"What's normal to you?"

"That's what I'm trying to find out."

He swallows. "Have you lost someone?"

"Not exactly."

He squints one eye at me.

I shrug. "Myself, I think."

"Ah." He looks out the window. "We all lose that, at some point though, right? We are strangers to ourselves every time we change."

His words cut right through me, so I ignore them. "Why do you have an identical tattoo as your brother if you don't miss him?"

He looks back at me. "I don't have to tell you that."

"You're right," I say. "But you could, if you wanted to." He kneads the back of his shoulder. He rubs the muscle for so long I worry I've ruined everything. I open my mouth to apologize but he cuts me off.

"My brother is a terror," he says.

I tilt my head. "But he wasn't always?"

With his fingers he rolls and unrolls the empty sugar packet on the table. "Not until my nephew died."

I regret asking the question. I wish he would swear or dump this latte over my head as punishment. But he only watches me, still as always. Somehow I know he's aware of what I want to ask and that I'm too cowardly to ask it.

"Yeah, it was on a boat," he says. "We took it out when I wasn't supposed to. But he wanted to learn how to water-ski. He kept asking and asking and after awhile it's impossible to say no to him, you would understand if you met him. He fell into the water. I don't want to say the rest. Anyway, my brother says it's my fault. It probably is. But I didn't want for it to happen, you know. I'm upset by it too. I barely eat or sleep. I don't know. He was only nine." He rubs his eye with the heel of his palm. "Are you fascinated yet?" He tries to smile but can't.

My whole body is tight with pain. "It isn't right, what he's saying."

"Yeah, okay."

"You know that?"

He avoids my eyes. "Sure."

"When did this happen?"

He exhales. "Last summer. It's why I'm here really. I needed to get away from it all." He picks at a loose thread on his jacket. "Didn't want to feel like a murderer any longer."

My mouth feels dry. I have to swallow before I can speak. "In the book it says we craft radical ideas to rationalize death. Because if we can't rationalize then we have to recognize that we don't have any control over it. That we are helpless to something bigger than ourselves."

"Hm."

"Maybe that's what your brother is doing. Not that it exonerates him."

"Yeah, maybe."

"Maybe that's what you're doing too. It's easier to believe it was your fault than believe you had no control at all."

He scratches the back of his head. "Why do you think you've lost yourself?"

"Done talking?"

He shrugs. "Don't really know why I said all that to be honest. I mean I don't even know you."

"Yeah," I say, my eyes fixed on his. "That's the only reason you're telling me."

He says nothing at first, disappears inside himself for a moment then nods.

"I like to pretend I'm other people," I say. "Real people I know or characters in my books. Like when I'm walking down the street or driving. I do it a lot. I can't remember now what my own opinions are and what I stole from someone else."

He rubs the rim of his coffee cup with his thumb. "I think you're nice enough as it is. No need to pretend to be someone else."

Heat blossoms across my cheeks. I desperately hope he doesn't notice. "Sometimes other people are a bit more interesting," I say.

"Yeah, I think we all feel like that though."

I probably should be irritated with his dismissal and yet it has the opposite effect.

He just made me feel normal.

The train grinds to a halt. He looks out the window then peers at his ticket.

"Yeah so, this is my stop."

My throat tightens. "Alright."

He gathers his bags and stands. He looks at me for a moment, obviously unsure what our parting should be. I don't offer him any help.

He touches my forearm. "I'm sorry your sister had a miscarriage."

"Me too."

I want to say I'm sorry about his nephew but he's already gone.

I remain on the train for another hour. I spend it staring out the window. I feel sad then feel stupid for it. When I arrive I check in to my hostel then wander around the city aimlessly. I drop coins into a busker's open guitar case. I order an Americano then throw it away after two sips. I think about how he called me nice enough. A pitiful compliment, but a compliment all the same. On Instagram, I post a picture of me in front of Rembrandt's former home and attach the location. I never do this, finding it gimmicky. But I feel the need to tether myself to something concrete. Now whenever people search for *Amsterdam* they will see my picture and know I exist. That I existed *here*. That I am something. A complete being. This knowledge soothes me.

That night, my head on a scratchy but pube-less pillowcase, I type *Brussels* into the search bar on Instagram and scroll through recent posts. There's one of a dark coffee drink sitting on top of a newspaper. The name is *leonard71*. My heart beats in my throat. I click on the profile. It's him. I scroll through his pictures, tapping on some and zooming in on his face. There aren't many, mostly just him with friends wearing jerseys for local sports teams. I scroll to the bottom and find one of his family. They are dressed in pastels. It's Easter. I zoom in on the little brown-haired boy in the front row.

Leonard's right.

I wouldn't be able to say no to him either.

A hot beat of moisture slips from my eye, creating a line down my cheek. I wipe it away, feeling foolish for crying about a stranger's death. I set my phone down and stare at the dark ceiling. Minutes pass. An hour. Suddenly, my phone dings. The waxy sheets crinkle as I sit up. Looking at the home screen I find an Instagram notification. Clicking on the banner, the screen opens up to the chat center where I have a new message from *leonard71*:

how were the pancakes?

Becoming South

Jenny Bates

Today, I called the checkout girl
at the local grocery store, *sweetheart*

she found a way to give me a discount
for bringing in my own wine bag

did not give up until she could get
that money off to be given

the day before Valentine's the man
in front of me, at this same store

bearded, big in overalls had only
two things in his cart

a bouquet of a dozen roses and
a large bag of dog food

I had alone things, wine, birdseed
and bags of peanut butter dog

treats I give to the Coyotes and
resident Raccoons

I gave that man my treat bags
Organic, Paul Newman and said

anyone who has only those two
things in his shopping cart

for Valentine's Day is ok by me —
the checkout girl, same one laughed

said I was so very kind, you see,
she knows me after twenty-two

years in this rural North Carolina
community I came to willingly

Do things for love, simple
random things, you won't regret

Owe your debts to goodwill
Even I can raise a glass to that.

Sending It Through

Emily Hall

The classroom had five pairs of chairs, each one facing a spinning wheel. On a table near the front were several braids of roving wool, some of which were dotted with blades of dried grass, while others were so delicate the light shone through the fibers. Julie, our instructor, told us as we filed in that either she or her aide Susan would be sitting beside us because learning to spin was tedious. Standing next to her own wheel, she invited us to take our seats. And even though I knew which chair was mine—there was a small bowl of wool alongside a list of directions on the left one—I hesitated. I was used to being the teacher, it was still strange to be the student.

This was the sixth art class that I had taken at a community art school since I had abruptly ended my career teaching college English. Over the past year, I plunged cotton fabric into an indigo vat; stripped willow leaves from branches while learning to naturally dye; and held thin sheets of copper over a gas flame to make earrings. Most often, those taking the classes with me were senior citizens who had waited to pursue the arts until they retired. They usually came with friends or relatives, but always included me in small talk, and only looked a bit curious about why someone in their mid-thirties was taking a class alone on a Thursday morning. I chose these classes aimlessly because I was trying to understand what I did and did not like. This was, after all, the driving force behind why I had quit teaching in the first place: after fourteen years doing it, I surprised myself one day when I realized I disliked it all along.

I had burned out, alongside so many other teachers, partly because of the pandemic, but mostly because teaching conditions had long felt untenable. In departmental faculty meetings, my colleagues would emphatically express their desire for students to be better supported. They asked *what else can we do* in eager, sincere tones. But when they asked this, I found myself instead assessing how much more I could give. I had taught hundreds of students a semester while on a one-year contract before being shifted to part-time because I had exceeded the number of years I was supposed to stay. During the last year I taught, I had no health insurance, so when a can lid sliced my finger open, I looked at the slick layers of fat inside the cut and wondered if I could just repair it myself.

It didn't help that I first came to teaching through strange circumstances. Three months after graduating with my undergraduate degree in English, the department chair called and offered me a position as an adjunct instructor in the very department from which I had just graduated. She had found a loophole where instructors could teach with only a bachelor's if they were pursuing a graduate degree, which I was. Because my only alternative was a cashier position at Wal-Mart, I accepted without considering what it would mean to teach college at twenty-two. She assured me that teaching would come naturally, told me to come pick up the books from her office, and explained that I'd start in three days, teaching some courses on the main campus and others on the nearby Air Force base.

When I arrived to teach my first class, I realized it was located in a small, closet-like room in the basement of the library. A large boiler rattled in the corner, and my students stared at me confused because their instructor was barely older than them. Like so many other adjuncts, I had no pedagogical training or support, and all semester I wrestled with classroom management problems. I fared better on the military base, where the students were eager-to-learn adults, but they were exhausted and traumatized from their recent tours in Afghanistan and Iraq. By December I was disoriented, and on the last day of class, a bookish girl named Raven lingered after class to ask compassionately, "Are you sure you even like doing this?" while I looked away and pushed forty research papers into my bag. The answer was "no," but I continued my teaching career anyway, leaving my position at the college for a steadier one at an impoverished public school before shifting back to teaching at a university.

Above all else, I taught because I didn't know an alternative path. I was from rural Delaware, and people in my family didn't go to college, least of all the women, who were encouraged to marry young and stifle their dreams. No one was happy when I majored in English, so teaching helped me reframe the usefulness of my degree. And although parts of it didn't suit my nature, I was forged into a teacher nonetheless. Over time, I tamed my natural impatience so I could sit in long periods of silence while students thought through challenging concepts. I infused my voice with empathy whenever a student realized his high school had not prepared him for the work we did in class, and I learned to cover and re-cover concepts students should have learned long ago. At times, this work was meaningful. When a cluster of shy girls came to my cubicle and pushed their friend forward so she could tell me my class made her love reading again, I was deeply moved. But in interviews for coveted tenure-track jobs, I could never sell my love for teaching. In one, the search committee members asked, not unkindly, if I'd be fully accessible to students upwards of twenty office hours of a week, something the department stipulated because the tuition was so high. I paused for a minute before saying "yes," but I knew they had seen doubt flicker across my face.

I was still in the process of shedding my teacherly identity, something that wasn't happening as quickly as I had assumed, when I began taking art classes. Being a student would create distance from my teacherly persona, I hoped, but when I attended my first class only three weeks after quitting my job, I teared up unexpectedly when the teacher wrote directions on the board. I slowly learned to quell my instinct to step in, especially when my confused classmates struggled, as I accepted that such intervention was no longer my responsibility. The side-by-side chairs in the spinning class felt like the ultimate challenge: here, I would just be a student, one who needed a lot of guidance.

As I slipped into my chair, Julie held up a journal. "All of you have one of these books under your seat. Go ahead and pick them up," she said. I found mine, a purple journal no bigger than my hand. "These have words of encouragement from students who've taken this class before," Julie clarified. "They're here to remind you that spinning yarn is challenging but you'll pick it up, just as the others did." Some of my classmates laughed nervously. "You want to know why I started these books?" Julie asked. We nodded yes. "Years ago, I taught spinning on a cruise ship, and one woman seemed annoyed, but refused my help several times when I offered it. Eventually, her friend complimented her work, and the woman spent the rest of the class smiling. When the class finished, I asked her if she had eventually found spinning meaningful, but she instead looked at me and said, 'It was your job to compliment me as I was learning. You're the teacher, after all.'" Julie paused for a minute, her blue eyes cast down towards the floor. "Consider these books proof of my encouragement," she softly concluded.

Julie then began the spinning demonstration. Her hands, heavily wrinkled and decorated with stacks of silver rings, moved deftly over all the parts of the wheel. Taking a long piece of wool, she tore part of it to show us how to test for staple length, the natural length of the fiber. She paused for a moment and invited us to do the same. We ripped our wool clumsily, holding it before our faces while fibers shed onto our laps. As Julie sat down in front of the wheel she reminded us that although our feet would want to race ahead, our hands would move more slowly. To achieve the perfect harmony that spinning wool requires we would have to make our hands, feet, and head work in unison.

I tied the long piece of roving wool onto my wheel, holding its gentle weight in my hand. As slowly as I could muster, I began to treadle, pushing my feet against the pedals of the wheel. Immediately, I over-twisted the wool as I tried to feed it through the wheel's orifice. An experienced spinner will slowly feed twisted wool through the orifice so it can wrap around the spindle, but my head couldn't seem to connect with my body, so I just kept twisting it until a spiraling braid of wool pooled in my left hand. Spotting my confusion, Susan quickly came over to sit next to me.

For two hours she worked with me, redirecting my hands when I mixed up how to hold the wool, and advising me to slow down my feet. Almost nothing worked. The length of overly-twisted yarn only grew, as did my impatience. Sweaty and frustrated, I told her I needed a break. I'd like to say that I brought the journal with all its words of encouragement with me, but I instead went to the bathroom and splashed water on my face, wishing I could just sneak out of the class and go home. Still, I steeled myself and went back into the classroom.

Returning to my chair, I told Susan, "I appreciate your help, but I think I need to figure this out on my own." She nodded and assured me that if I wanted her help, I could just call her over. Picking up the overly-twisted yarn, I sat in front of the wheel, determined to teach myself how to spin. I spent thirty minutes slowly familiarizing myself with the wheel, hoping I would understand it better. But as I continued to struggle, Julie came over, frowning. "You've overly twisted your yarn," she told me, pointing to the mess in my hand. "See all the energy that twist has? It will affect the rest of the wool if you don't fix it."

I laughed anxiously and admitted I didn't know what to do. Julie looked at me calmly before saying, "You've got to send it through. Quick as lightning. Don't try to hold it, just send it through." But I wasn't sure what this meant. "Pedal your feet as quickly as you can," she instructed. "Send it through like lightning," she repeated. I did as she told me, racing as I pedaled, while the braid of wool rapidly coiled around the spindle like a lumpy snake. With the overly-twisted yarn out of my hands, the remaining wool suddenly became easy to work with. For a second, I understood how to make my hands, feet, and mind work in unison. One hand softly held the wool lightly while the other slowly fed it into the orifice.

"Look," Julie breathed, "You are *spinning*." Her eyes beamed, but I lost faith in my hands and tangled the wool once more.

Moments before the class had started, Julie and I had talked one-on-one about teaching. I accidentally came to the art center early, so she and I ate an impromptu lunch together, and although we were strangers we curiously felt like old friends. When she discovered that I had recently stopped teaching, she didn't make the usual comments I had from others who were perplexed that I would forgo my "free" summers and the supposedly lavish lifestyle of a professor. Instead, she asked directly, but quietly, "how did you get to the point that you had to leave?"

Because she had asked so plainly, and no one else had ever asked me this before, I told her what I so rarely told others: "I was walking around my neighborhood one evening, and I realized that the person who went to teach each week was actually me. At some point, I had numbed myself to the job so badly that I thought of her as a separate person, someone else who absorbed students' anger when they couldn't make up an entire semester's worth of late work, or who had to intervene when students said hateful things to their classmates because they were emboldened by politics. I was sick every morning driving to work but thought this was normal until the pandemic began and it stopped."

I paused for a moment before adding, "But leaving higher education is deeply taboo, and even though this was the best possible choice for me, I still feel a little ashamed."

Julie nodded knowingly, "I taught special education for thirty years. I was lucky in the sense that I loved my students, but getting to those thirty years took so much work, and most days I just didn't want to go in. I'm still nervous every time I teach. Even this spinning wheel class—well, the nerves never fade," she sighed. We both stayed silent for a minute, the heaviness of teaching sitting stone-like in the middle of our table.

As I tangled my yarn on the wheel beside her, Julie reached out and grabbed my hand, peeling back my ring finger and pinkie, which were tightly holding onto the wool. "You can't overthink this," she whispered. She was right. I once again found my groove, sending the wool through with ease as I carefully treadled. "She's spinning!" Julie cried with delight, clapping her hands. "Yeah, look at her go!" Susan cheered. With both of them watching me, I stumbled again, over-twisting the yarn and forgetting to send it through. "You've got to just let it go," Julie told me, her eyebrows contracting with sympathy. And even though I knew her advice was too on the nose, it didn't make my heart ache any less.

As the class wrapped up, I slowly became more familiar with the wheel and the meditative state it demanded. I finished my first awkward skein of homespun and, at Julie's request, selected another ball of roving so I could continue to practice. Using a delicate, brown skein of merino that caught my eye, I spun the second skein more capably than the first. After she finished working with one of my classmates, Julie came over and patiently held both my skeins while I plied them together, and when I finished, she held the yarn up and showed me that it naturally fell into a soft loop. "You did it!" she exclaimed. "It's not overly twisted. In fact, it came out nicely balanced after all."

To me, the yarn looked chunky and unwieldy, nothing like the skeins I bought in stores, but I smiled anyway and gathered my things to leave before Julie explained we weren't finished yet. "There's a graduation ceremony," she explained. "Because you've graduated from a novice to a knowledgeable spinner." She pointed to a gray bag and asked Susan to get the medals.

I walked over to where Susan was laying several nylon necklaces with salt-dough medallions across the table. "Pick whichever one you want," Julie instructed, as she grinned and nibbled on a snack.

Emily Hall **59**

The medallions were painted different colors but all of them said the same thing: "I Spin," along with the date, November 2023. I selected a moss green one, hesitating because I felt a little silly going through with the ritual. But then I remembered that if nothing else, a graduation ceremony recognizes the end of something. I handed Susan my selection and leaned forward while she placed it around my neck. Julie snipped the first few inches of my handspun yarn and tucked the brown tuft into the jump ring on my medallion. "Your diploma," she said, before she opened her arms to hug me.

The Bird Whisperer

Susan Woods Morse

She told me that an owl came and sat at her feet
silently waiting for her to finish morning coffee
how he twisted his head looking up at her
and then silently flew to his perch
and later when a small blackbird hit the window
of her house, lying stunned, perhaps wondering
about life and its mysteries
how she stroked its back over and over
repeating *be free, be free*
and it rose up and flew like a goddamned Christ figure
over the backyard fence.

She has many more bird stories—
but the one she loves best of all is reciting
her mantra about the blue heron,
legs tucked and trailing behind its lithe body,
how it silently wings overhead on stilled afternoons,
casually dispersing the clouds in her mind—

a mystery how it knows the sure path
to the river and how to keep it all flowing.

At the Stanford Mall

Joyce Schmid

Palo Alto, California

As if I am about to die,
I see my life—

the people shopping back and forth
intent on lattés, ice creams, and designer jeans—

or is it the afterlife I see
as if through Dante's eyes

the way I did in Reno, when I saw
the shades condemned to slot machines?

But here between the concrete walkways
someone put their hands in soil—

and planted poppies, zinnias,
and birds of paradise.

Green hummingbirds discover them
and pump their hungry tongues inside

to feed on nectar, hovering
on wings no one can see.

In Time You Will Understand

Robert Wallace

My mother came into my bedroom on the morning of my eleventh birthday completely naked. Not a stitch on her. I was awake but still in bed. She sat on the edge of the bed and bent over my prostrate body, her breasts hanging above my face like misshapen water balloons.

"Mama, you're naked," I said.

She put her finger to her lips. "Shush," she said. "Hurry up and get dressed."

"Why?"

"Just get dressed. Meet me in the kitchen in five minutes." She stood up, and I was tempted to cover my eyes. "And Lorna," she said. "Be quiet about it. I don't want to wake your father."

When I arrived downstairs a little more than five minutes later she was standing in the kitchen, looking out the window above the sink. She had a cup of coffee in her hand, and she was fully dressed. She turned around and handed me her coffee cup. Her eyes looked spacious and jittery.

"I hope you didn't wake your father. I want to be out of here before he wakes up."

I didn't tell her, before walking downstairs, that I had stopped at his bedroom door. I was tempted to wake him, but I didn't want to upset my mother. I hadn't a notion what she might do. But I had written out a note and slipped it under his door.

"Let's go," my mother said. "Things to do and places to go."

The sun was coming up as we walked to the car. I felt a chill in the air, and I quickly went back into the house and grabbed my coat. I also grabbed my mother's coat, throwing both of them into the backseat.

"Where are we going?" I asked.

"You'll see."

"Give me a hint."

"No," my mother said.

She revved the car before pulling out of the driveway.

It was a little after 7:00 on a Saturday. The streets were mostly empty. A few dog walkers, not much else. My mother sped through our little town in the foothills of North Carolina as if she was trying to escape. I didn't say anything, but I hoped a police car would spot her speeding and pull her over, but when we passed the sign that said "Come Again" she suddenly slowed down. She exhaled.

"Mama, where are we going?" I asked.

"Lorna," she said. "You're not to ask me that question again. You here?"

"Yes," I said.

I looked at my mother. She was wearing a loud blouse and jeans, and black sneakers. Her hair was uncombed, and bits of lint was in it. There were dark circles under her eyes. She tapped the steering wheel with her right forefinger.

My mother lit a cigarette, and the car filled up with smoke. I kept my head turned, looking out the window, watching the telephone poles and the small, mostly sad white house's drift speedily backward. Patches of dirty snow collected around the poles from the snowstorm that happened several days ago. The heater in the car was going full blast, and it made a racket like a blender when first turned on. Still, it was mostly putting out lukewarm air.

"Would you like some music?" my mother asked.

"No," I said.

"News?"

My mother reached for the radio dial.

"Nope," I said.

"Don't say 'nope' Lorna. It's lazy English."

"Sorry," I said. "What I wish is that I had brought a book to read."

When she snuffed out her cigarette, I watched it smolder in the overflowing ashtray before a last-ditch stream of smoke snaked its way toward me. I opened the window slightly and let the smoke escape.

"What are you reading now?"

"Flannery O'Connor," I said. "Her stories."

"Good choice, Lorna," she said. "Unexpected violence can be enthralling. You must read Shirley Jackson next. For someone truly enigmatic."

There was little traffic on the road. Clouds filled the sky, and the late March weather had the look of winter instead of spring. Mother turned off Highway 226, and we got behind a slow-moving truck that had a coarse-looking cloth covering the bed. One corner of the cloth flapped wildly, and I could see old furniture in the bed. A large gnome stood straight up in the corner where the cloth fluttered in the breeze. I expected my mother to get antsy driving behind the truck, but she seemed content to keep her distance and not try to pass. When the truck pulled off to allow us to go by, she pulled in behind the truck, and quickly exited the car.

"You stay in the car, Lorna," she said.

I rolled my window down. My mother walked up to the driver's side of the truck and knocked on the window. While she waited for the driver to respond, I retrieved her purse from behind her seat. I opened it up to see if she had brought her pills. Her wallet was in there, two tubes of lipstick, several wadded-up tissues, and a handful of unwrapped Certs. But no pills. It had been over a year since her last episode, but I feared she was having one now. The last one lasted several weeks. She had left the house then and had driven all the way to Florida, calling from the Gulf Coast after disappearing for several days. She had always disappeared by herself. The fact that I was with her—if she was having an episode—was something new.

A large man got out of the truck. He stood at least a foot taller than my mother. His red beard hung down to his chest. He walked to the back of the truck, my mother following right behind him. They looked at the gnome. The paint was chipped and shreds of it hung from the gnome like weathered paint on a house. The tip of its nose was broken, exposing the gray concrete. My mother was talking to the large man, but I couldn't make out what she was saying. Finally the man pulled the gnome out of the truck and walked it back to our car. I rolled my window up some. My mother opened the trunk and the man put the gnome in it. The rear of the car immediately dropped a few inches.

"Hand me my purse, Lorna," my mother said.

She was on my side of the car. I opened the door and gave her the purse.

"This is my daughter, Lorna," my mother said. "This here is Lars."

"Hello," I said.

Lars didn't say anything. His lips were the only thing visible, and he kept them together, so I couldn't even see his teeth.

"Thank you," my mother said. "Fifty dollars."

Lars nodded but didn't say anything. He took the money, looked at me one more time in a way that made me turn my head. He then walked to his truck, got in, and drove off.

When my mother got back into the car at first she didn't say anything. She got out a tube of lipstick from her purse and rapidly smeared it across her lips, leaving a red mark on her cheek in each corner of her mouth.

"Happy birthday," she finally said. "That's your birthday present."

"What? The gnome?"

"Of course."

"What am I going to do with a giant gnome?"

"Use your imagination, Lorna." She pulled back on the road, and we continued on our way. "When we get home, we'll clean it up. Repaint it."

"What about the nose?"

"We'll get some cement and mold us a new nose," my mother said. "When we're all done you can put it in your room."

"My room? What would I want with a gnome in my room?"

"A gnome has magical powers, Lorna. It will protect you."

"I need to be protected in my own room?"

My mother turned her head and looked at me with squinty eyes. "Yes," she said. "We all need protection, Lorna. Especially in our rooms."

As we made our way up a mountain, the car rumbling like it was telling us to stop, I could feel the air outside getting colder even though the faulty heater was going full blast. Air entered the car at every unsealed opening, making a motley crew of whistling sounds. The air inside the car smelled like a wet, wool sweater.

After a time we started down the mountain, and my mother kept tapping her brakes and soon they started to squeal. The brakes smelled like burning hair. We were entering the town of Spruce Pine. There was an impatient driver behind us, and I turned to look but my mother told me not to turn around. Soon he sped by us and beeped his horn.

"Bastard," my mother said.

She pulled into a parking lot, coasting the car right up near the door of a brewery.

I looked at my mother. She lit another cigarette. Finally she turned the ignition off. It was 9:30, and my stomach was growling because I hadn't eaten any breakfast.

"Mama," I said. "Are you all right?"

But my mother didn't say anything. She leaned her seat back and smoked with her eyes closed.

I stepped out of the car. I put my coat on and walked up to the brewery. It was closed, but when I peered through the window I could see a man behind the counter. He was busy emptying a dishwasher full of glasses. I walked around to the back of the building where there was a large dumpster. Broken bottles of beer were strewn all around the metal container. The sun, which had suddenly appeared, reflected off some of the broken green glass. The odor of something rotten, like a dead animal had gotten into the dumpster, filled my nostrils.

Laying against the outside of the brewery was a homeless man. Slowly he rose, stumbled, and started walking toward me. Suddenly he sped up, and he was in front of me even as I moved to avoid him.

"Wait," he said. "Do you have any money?"

"Leave me alone," I said.

"I won't hurt you."

He reached out and grabbed the sleeve of my coat, but I jerked my arm away and ran off. When I got back to the car, my mother wasn't inside. I looked back to see if the homeless man was following me, but I didn't see him. I didn't see my mother anywhere. I started walking toward where I could see other buildings. It was a long street with houses on both sides. Some of the houses had been turned into retail shops. One house was painted a lime-green color. There were windchimes hanging from tree limbs and crystals that were spinning in the breeze that hung from large metal hooks attached to places on the porch.

The shop looked like a place my mother would like, so I went inside. She was standing just inside the door. She had sandalwood incense in her hand, and she was holding it to her nose, deeply sniffing it.

"Mama," I said.

"Lorna."

"You left me."

"Oh, I would never do that. I knew we'd fine each other."

She shuffled over to a corner of the house that displayed pottery. There were pots with faces, grimacing old men with cowboy mustaches, creepy-looking women with their eyes closed, gray faces with google-eyed expressions and protruding teeth.

The house was dimly lit. Candles were burning in several places: vanilla and patchouli scented the air, and some other fragrance I couldn't name, something pungent and honed.

In another room, a much smaller room, I could see a boy or a young man—I couldn't tell which—standing behind a counter. He was in formal wear, not exactly a tuxedo, but something like it, a dark jacket with a similar colored bowtie. He saw me looking at him. He smiled. Then he came around the counter. As he approached, I saw he was wearing hard-soled shoes. They looked black and shiny.

"Is there something I can help you with?" he asked.

I noticed a wisp of hair above his lip. His dark hair was combed back and moussed.

"I don't know, "I said.

I didn't know what else to say, so I told him it was my birthday. He smiled again.

"Happy birthday," he said.

"She's twelve today," my mother said.

She had walked up behind me and put her hands on my shoulder. I didn't correct her about my age.

"Nice suit," my mother said.

"Blame it on my little sister," he said. "She likes me to dress up. She has this doll named Isobel and when you pull the doll's string it says, 'I love you.' She likes to pretend I'm marrying Isobel."

I looked out one of the back windows of the house. The sky was spitting snow now.

"You want anything else?" the boy asked.

"What?" my mother said.

The boy looked at the incense my mother still held in her hand.

"That's a nice scent," he said.

"Not unless you have something that goes with a large gnome," my mother said.

"A gnome," the boy said. "As a matter of fact we have a garden section out back."

My mother and I followed the boy out the back entrance. On the way he said his name was Jimmy but that most people called him Jim.

"What's your middle name?" my mother asked.

"Aaron," he said.

"I think I'll call you Aaron," my mother said.

I was glad to see that my mother was wearing her coat because when we went outside it felt like the temperature had dropped a few degrees. The backyard had paths made from tree bark. There were lanterns on large wrought-iron poles, Japanese-style lanterns made of paper in various colors, and other outdoor lighting strung around, including globes of glass over brass-colored mermaids that were lit by candles. The sky was cloud covered, so the lights gave off a feel of twilight.

My mother gravitated to an area underneath a blossoming redbud tree. Discarded purple blossoms were scattered underneath the tree like confetti. Strewn underneath and in the tree were small—no more than a few inches—figures, including some children, each wearing dresses and holding gardening tools. Near the display were a couple of incandescently-green Adirondack chairs. My mother sat in one, and she stared at the figures, like she was studying them.

"They're all female," my mother finally said.

"Yes," the boy said.

"What are they?" I asked.

"They're called gnomess," my mother said. "Female gnomes."

My mother kneeled on the ground. She picked up one of the female gnomes. Then she handed it to me. It was made of terracotta clay, painted in bright yellow.

"These are beautiful," my mother said. "But I prefer to call them fairies."

I looked at Jim. He had his hands in his pocket, but when I reached to give him the gnome, he took the gnome in both of his hands, and I felt the tips of his fingers softly touch my hand.

Robert Wallace **69**

"I'll take them all," my mother said.

When we got back to the car, my mother put the female gnomes in a cardboard box in the trunk. We walked inside the brewery, past an older couple who were sitting near the front. They both shivered when the door was opened. We found a booth near the rear of the restaurant. The seats were made of green vinyl, partially repaired with Duct Tape that someone had colored with a green crayon.

We ordered a large pizza with pepperoni and mushrooms. My mother ordered a beer. I hadn't seen my mother drink alcohol in a long time. I looked at her as she took a sip of her beer, closing her eyes. Her face got all dreamy, and she didn't open them until she took another swallow.

"Mama, are you off your pills?" I asked.

"That's my business, Lorna," she said. "Sometimes you act like you're my mother."

When the pizza came, I removed the mushrooms and started eating. My mother picked at her pizza, and I was through my third slice before she had eaten even half of one. She took a piece of paper out of her pocket and began writing down numbers. The same numbers over and over again, adding them up as if she expected to get a different result.

"What are you doing?" I asked.

"Just eat your pizza, Lorna," she said.

I swallowed some Coca-Cola. I ate another slice of pizza, and watched my mother fill the paper until the numbers overlapped each other.

"I'd like to call Father," I said. "Can we find a phone."

"What for?" my mother said. "I know you left a note for him."

My mother looked at me as if she was looking right through me. I stared at her. "You didn't say anything against leaving him a note," I said. "You only said not to wake him."

"I'm not mad," she said.

"Don't you think he might be worried."

"Look, Lorna. Your father is a good man. But he's kind of conservative, you know."

"What is that supposed to mean?"

"He's rather plain. Good but plain."

"If we had a cell phone," I said. "We could call him."

"Cell phones are an abomination. They'll take your soul from you."

"It's 2010, Mama."

My mother drank the last of her beer. She slapped a twenty-dollar bill on the table.

"I've been thinking what I would miss in this world if I were to leave it," she said.

"Are you leaving it?" I asked.

"We all have to leave it sometime."

"I don't understand."

"In time you will, Lorna. In time you will."

We pulled out of the parking lot of the brewery, my mother hell bent, it seemed, in driving as fast as she could up the mountain toward the town of Little Switzerland. I tried to calm my own brain. It felt on fire, like I suspected her brain was—I imagined little voices inside her head speaking all at once, and her having no idea which one to listen to, each telling her to do a catalogue of things.

It was a fifteen-minute drive up to Little Switzerland. We drove it in ten. Somehow my mother kept the car on the road, although at one point she swerved into the other lane just as another vehicle was coming down the mountain. I screamed. The car horn from the other vehicle blared like a whistle on a train. My mother turned the car just in time, missing the other car, but she overcompensated, scraping against an outcrop of rock. The passenger-side door, along the seam, buckled. The sound of ripping metal didn't stop my mother from moving forward. There was no place to pull over anyway. As we neared the top of the mountain and the village of Little Switzerland, my mother attempted to floor the car. Fortunately the engine didn't respond, and we sputtered to a stop right in front of Books and Beans.

We sat there a moment, quiet, and I vowed to myself that after I exited the car I wouldn't get back in the car again.

"Well, here we are," my mother said.

I tried the door, but it wouldn't open. I crawled over the seat and got out through the backdoor. My heart was galloping like a race horse's. My mother came around the car and looked at me as if nothing had happened. She didn't look at the crushed door.

"Shall we go in," my mother said.

"You almost got us killed," I said.

"That's a bit of an exaggeration," she said.

"What?" I said. "Look at the door."

"It's just a scratch."

"Mama, that's not just a scratch. The door will no longer open."

She had her purse in her hand. She opened it and pulled out two twenty-dollar bills and handed them to me. Her eyes were blinking like an emergency vehicle. Then she opened the trunk and took out the box of fairies.

"Go buy yourself some books," my mother said. "I'm going to find a bathroom."

There have been times during my life when I have tried to bend my mind toward fantasy. I tried to do that now even as I watched my mother walk down the road, holding the box of female gnomes, and away from me. I closed my eyes. I imagined the whole day had been a dream. I was at home in bed, and my mother and father were in the other room, asleep. and my mother's pills were on the bedside table, left there from when she had taken one the night before. But when I opened my eyes, I caught a glimpse of my mother just as she walked around the corner of the Little Switzerland hotel, and then she reappeared farther up the hill, her body bent over to accommodate the incline, and then she disappeared into a stand of fir trees.

The trunk was still open. I searched inside it for a sharp instrument. But other than the giant gnome, there was little to be found, not even a spare tire. But inside the car I found a straight-head screwdriver. I jabbed at one of the rear tires, trying my best to puncture it, but the screwdriver wasn't sharp enough. A large piece of metal hung near the handle of the buckled door. I jabbed at it with the screwdriver. It made an awful sound. It was cold outside, and my hands were freezing. Finally, exasperated at how difficult it was to break off the piece of metal, I grabbed it and pulled. I felt my skin tear. But it loosened enough so that after a few more strikes with the screwdriver, the piece dropped to the pavement. I ignored the stinging in my right palm. There was an old, greasy rag in the trunk. I wrapped the piece of metal in the rag and did my best to slice the tire, scraping across the sidewall multiple times. I couldn't tell if it had any effect, but I hoped in time to see the tire loose air. I was determined not to let my mother drive again.

I wiped my bloody hand with the rag the best I could. I found a few crumpled up tissues in the car and I pressed the tissues tightly against the cut until there were only a few oily beads of blood. I then went inside the bookstore and asked the clerk if I could use the phone. I called my father, and the phone rang several times, and I was about to give up when he finally answered. I started crying right away. I wanted to sound older, and I tried to explain everything in a calm, adult manner, but hearing his voice gave me such relief that it was the hope associated with the relief that unleased something in me.

"Lorna," my father said. "Just tell me where you're."

"We're in Little Switzerland," I said. "The car's parked in front of the bookstore."

"Okay. Stay by the car. I'll be there in less than an hour."

I waited by the car, swiveling my head back and forth between looking for my father's car coming up the road, and where I had last seen my mother disappear. The relief I felt talking to my father quickly dissipated because the wait seemed interminable, and my worry for my mother grew and grew. What could she be doing? And why did she take the female gnomes with her?

I was about to go looking for her when my father finally arrived.

"Lorna," my father said when he got out of the car.

I started crying again. He took me in his arms, and I wanted nothing more than to stay there forever. He was wearing his full-size peacoat, and my father's arms felt steady and warm.

"I'm sorry," I said.

"Never mind," my father said. "Where's your mother?"

"She's off her pills," I said.

"I know. We need to get her to a hospital. Where is she?"

I pointed past the hotel. "I last saw her enter the woods up by the hotel."

"Show me," he said.

I took off running. My father ran with me. It was hard going because we were running up hill. My father's breaths came in heavy loud bursts, but he didn't tell me to stop. When we got up to where I thought she had gone into the woods I slowed down and waited for my father to catch his breath.

"In here," I said.

There was a poorly used trail, and we walked in for thirty yards, my father leading the way. We stepped on last fall's leaves and pine needles. When it looked like the trail ended, my father stopped. We listened for her. I looked on the ground for something, anything that would indicate she had been here. And that's when I saw the fairy. It was barely visible, a small head protruding above a small rock.

"This way," I said.

We bushwacked through the trees. Along the way I scooped up the gnome and stuck it in my coat pocket. We made our way slowly, clearing away branches with our arms, ducking under others.

After a few minutes, my father said, "Are you sure this is the right way, Lorna?"

"No," I said.

We trudged on for several more minutes, until we came to a small clearing that overlooked the mountains. My mother was there, laying on the ground, about ten feet from the precipice, all the fairies surrounding her,. She wasn't wearing her coat, but she had covered herself with it like a blanket. She appeared to be asleep. I could see her shallow breaths rise and fall. I thought about what my mother once said to me. "Sleep is an odd thing," she said. "It's like you're there and not there." My father and I didn't say anything. We were quiet, just watching her sleep, when she suddenly awoke, like she sensed we were observing her.

"Lorna," she said. "Richard."

She didn't seem surprised to see my father.

She stood up. Her coat fell off her. Pine needles clung to her ankles. She picked up one of the fairies and flung it over the mountain. "You're free," she said. Carefully, she picked up each of them, tossing them over the precipice and into the air. They seemed to fly into the sky as if they had wings. I didn't hear the fairies crashing below. They flew into the air, each of them, and they made no sound, as if they didn't fall from the sky. There was only the sound of a hawk screeching high above us. With each toss my mother moved closer and closer to the edge of the overhang. I looked at my father, but he didn't move. "Shouldn't we get her," I said.

"No," my father said.

There was a crease in his forehead. Weariness shown about his face. He stood there, rocking back and forth on his heels, as if he, too, was standing on the edge of some precipice. He raised his arms and closed his eyes and began flapping his arms as if he wanted to take flight. Then he quickly opened his eyes, and he stared at me.

"You're bleeding," my father said.

I looked at my hand. Somewhere along the way I had lost the soiled tissues. My hand was still bleeding some, and the fresh blood mixed with the dried blood and the grease from the soiled rag.

"Yes," I said.

"I'm sorry," my father said. "For everything."

Out beyond where my mother stood clouds were forming. They were big fluffy clouds with tinges of black along their edges. Other clouds, smaller ones, were surrounding the big clouds. They looked like they were marching, as if they had some place to be and the big clouds were in their way. More clouds suddenly rushed in and the whole sky looked like a herd of elephants. When I looked back at my father I saw that he was gazing at the massing clouds. The side of his face twitched a moment. Something shifted in me just then, and I felt that I suddenly didn't understand either of my parents. My father turned his head in my direction just as a bit of plum-colored light shone in the sky.

"What do you see in the clouds?" I asked.

"Cake," he said.

"What?"

"And candles." He smiled. "Happy birthday," my father said.

My mother was standing inches from the edge, looking like she was about to pitch over. When my father faithfully walked toward her and took her in his arms, my mother's arms went straight in the air, and I thought she was going to hit him. He picked her up, cradling her. Then he put her down. When they walked by me, my father was hugging my mother's waist.

"I'm not someone you can own," she whispered.

"I never thought so," my father said.

It was a long time before I turned and followed them.

About Time Stopping

Hugh Burke

A moon glimpsed
through banisters of cloud.
A spry little face caught peering
down on all the unquiet. I wonder,
What will satisfy us?

An asked for name
spelled instead of spoken: "M.i.c.a.h."
A chat about time stopping.
Like the stone, I am thinking
as I spell mine in return
Who is like God?

Meanwhile, the miser counts his coins.
Palms heavy with soil,
he brushes each one into being.
Paying attention, not to their value,
but to the oblivion they pierce —
savoring their pale, nourishing gleam.
Like glimpsed moons, they rise
from the vague, uncertain ground.
One at a time, he returns them
to their secret tombs.
What would he lose?

May we too remain curious
far beyond our bedtimes.
May we reinter our coins.
May we give certainty a wide berth,
shatter our names
into unintelligible shards.
For, rather than in greeting,
it's from the apogee where desire murmurs

her most sublime answer:
No one. Nothing.

A Poem Should Come Like This

Susan Woods Morse

Those are the best ones   the lush ones,
        illumined phrases
                and memories full of moonlight
                        right now
autumn berries that maybe the fox found this morning—

quick tug and snip   crunching them off the vine,
        his lips pulled in a smiling half snarl
                as he reaches upwards
and then his tongue
                his tongue
                        delicately swirls the black berry juice.
Perhaps he might not eat again for a while.

Hunting can be sparse any time of year,
        just so with poems,
                but especially with winter beginning to loom
                        in upon the clouds.

No words for me today. Darkness comes early.
                By 5 p.m. I no longer hope to see you
though I might hear you
                        trudging
                                up the long, muddy road,
                                        you of little language,
        weighed down
by all those words you never utter,

the ones you long to unburden, to scatter—

like licking burrs from a tail   your tongue catching
        on the little sharp points.

But morning always breaks again. The sun strikes a balance;
        it cups piercing light
            and a small forgiveness round as berries.

It's Called Spam

CM Kelly

"Back in the day …." I realize that such an opening leads one to some preconceived conclusion about what will follow, so my challenge is to shake up your preconceived thought with a light, maybe funny, and somewhat educational story.

In the late 1960s, we moved from a 3 bedroom apartment in Scranton PA to a farmhouse built in the 1800s on a dirt road, just a few miles outside of town. For some unknown reason living on a paved versus dirt road was a differentiator in one's social standing. I never knew why, but in those years it made sense. Apparently, in the 1950s or thereabouts, the farmhouse was converted into a hunting cabin or club, thus it had the modern conveniences of electricity and indoor plumbing. When we moved in, the house underwent a major renovation — or more of an overhaul. New roof, windows, wiring, plumbing, floors, furnace, well, septic system, the works.

With the farmhouse came a few acres of land, more than enough room to allow the nine of us with space to play kickball, baseball, and football. At one point our dad put up a crude basketball court made from a pair of four-by-fours and a piece of plywood. The combo grass-dirt court was easy on falls but made dribbling quite a challenge. Between the house and the land came a list of never-ending chores, ranging from cutting grass to painting fences, trimming trees and bushes to hand digging the basement, the latter being a story itself.

With open fields on all sides, a small creek in the backyard, two ponds just a stone's throw away, and tall pine trees in the front yard, this old farmhouse was the idyllic place to raise a family of nine children. With great pride, our mother declared, "We live on Windrift Acres." I recall how proudly she put up a hand-painted sign on the corner pine tree stating so.

I don't know if it was my dad's or mom's idea, but right after we bought the farmhouse, we constructed a 20x15 family room addition with tall windows overlooking the creek and ponds and a fireplace at the other end. The room, of course was trimmed in 1960s wood paneling, provided our Irish clan of 11 much-needed elbow room. I can safely say that this room was pretty much built with child labor. There would be many projects at this home homestead that didn't just build muscles, but also character. Since the kitchen was rather small, the family room became the center point of the household. Of course, the one TV we owned resided in this room.

In Archie Bunker fashion, my father had his favorite chair right in front of the TV (for Gen X and Millennials, think of Sheldon's spot from the *Big Bang Theory*). This family room brought us together for the nightly, post-dinner tradition of watching TV shows. Of course, living in a remote area meant we were lucky to get one TV station, so our viewing choices weren't just limited; they didn't exist. My father initiated the original channel surfing by having one of us 6 boys climb up on the roof and turn the antenna until a station was found.

To complete the setting, we were a family of modest financial means, strong in character and honesty but always light with the dollars.

So, on to the main topic: "It's called SPAM." Although the family room was the center of activity, we had all our meals in the kitchen. For such a large family, I don't know how my mom got by with just a basic stove with one oven and a refrigerator the size you'd find today in a garage. No microwave or dishwasher, just a well-used two-slice toaster. Due to the size of the kitchen and because of our financial condition, the kitchen table was a picnic table we moved from the porch, the old wooden kind you would find in a park. My mother hated it. The kitchen door was the main entrance to the house, and the picnic table was the first thing any visitor would see, a telltale sign of our economic standing.

With nine children, mealtime at our house looked more like a cafeteria than a homey Norman Rockwell painting. Breakfast was a procession of children running through the process of taking showers, brushing teeth, checking the dryer for clean clothes, and finding lost shoes, or coats. Most of us would wolf down a bowl of cereal while others would grab a few pieces of toast, of course, they had to have cinnamon sugar on top of them. We were essentially on our own while our mom was busy making the batches of peanut butter and jelly sandwiches for our lunches. The process was loosely choreographed to get the *troops* to the front gate before the school bus arrived. Only on Sunday did breakfast differ. Because we were all headed to the same Mass, it was the only time we had Mom and Dad join us for breakfast. Mom would cook Dad his eggs and bacon while the rest of us did the cereal/toast routine. Once in a great while, Mom would make scrambled eggs for the children, a treat generally reserved for holidays or birthdays.

Lunches were the standard peanut butter and jelly sandwiches, sometimes just peanut butter or just jelly, but never cold cuts with cheese. I don't recall anything else in the brown paper bags we took to school for 12 years, but we might have an occasional cupcake or celery sticks. When we got older and attended high school, we were allowed to buy a cafeteria lunch once per week. What a treat that was. I don't remember the price of the cafeteria food, but I do recall a milk carton costing six cents and an ice cream sandwich a dime.

Dinners were less confusing than breakfast. During the week and on Saturdays, most of the nine were either at a sporting event, Scouts, or catechism classes. Thus, the "school night" seating around the picnic table was rarely maxed out. Those of us getting home after 6:00 p.m. were usually faced with dried-out, overcooked leftovers. Sunday was more traditional, with the whole household sitting down for a chicken dinner with vegetables and mashed potatoes. Of course, all dinners started with reciting Grace; we sat up straight, chewed with our mouths closed, spoke when spoken to, and asked to be excused from the table.

Mom did have her routine: Sunday was almost always a chicken dinner, Wednesday was spaghetti night, Friday was either pizza or a tuna noodle casserole (never meat on a Friday), and Saturday was hamburgers with oven-baked french fries. As you can surmise, our mother did not do elaborate or detailed cooking; how could she with such a large crew and a two to three-hour serving window?

I remember some aspects of dinner at Windrift Acres that are noteworthy, like having scrambled eggs with cut-up hotdogs for dinner, opening can after can of apple sauce, and boiling potatoes in what resembled a five-gallon painter's bucket and the mountain of potato skins that came with it. One staple in almost every meal — a taste and image that still runs a cold shiver down my spine — was the yellow wax beans heaped on our plates.

We never had fancy meals growing up. Thanksgiving Day turkey and Christmas Day ham were once-a-year events, and those dinners, in many ways, did resemble a Norman Rockwell painting. Funny side note: In the 1970s, with the skyrocketing prices of beef there was a nationwide beef embargo, well this didn't impact my family. The only red meat we had was the lowest-grade hamburger or something called a cube steak.

The one dinner I painfully remember was when Mom cooked up some pan-fried canned ham (i.e., SPAM) and mashed potatoes with those yellow beans. In the 1970s, canned hams were the "in thing." Mom convinced us, or at least me, that the canned ham was akin to a Christmas Day ham.

Years later, while in college, I had breakfast in a diner with a friend. I ordered fried ham and scrambled eggs special. With just one bite, I recognized the ham on my plate. I mentioned to my friend sitting in the booth with me that this restaurant served the expensive fried ham my mother served us at home. He immediately broke into a burst of deep, prolonged laughter and told me that the fried ham next to my eggs was fried SPAM. He explained what he thought SPAM was made of, which I won't repeat here.

A range of emotions went through me. First, I was embarrassed by my social standing for thinking that SPAM was an expensive ham. Yes, even at college I was still the green hick raised on a dirt road in the mountains of Pennsylvania.

The second, more powerful emotion was that my mom duped me, a concept I could never accept. While growing up, our mother repeatedly told us, "You're as good as any of those other children, no matter what they say, think, or wear." Whether we wore hand-me-down clothes, hitchhiked to and from events, drove in outdated-rusted cars, or had to get a paying job as soon as we got our driving learner's permit, our mother consistently drove into us, that people with money were no better than me, my brothers or sisters. She established a core value that character matters the most, not what you wear, what you drive, the size of your home, or how much money you have.

Getting over this emotional disappointment took a while, but in the end, I had to admit that Mom duped me. SPAM was not a fancy, expensive, imported ham. I've rationalized this memory by believing that my ever-optimistic mother was just making lemonade out of lemons.

About Bad News

John J. Hohn

The afternoon ached with fatigue,
flaccid as a fat woman's arm
resting on a tabletop—
defiant of anything, just anything
that would promise
reprieve and serve up
a little contentment.

Once assured of my strength—
An arm?
God, yes.
I could throw rocks
at the stars
and hit one now and then.
Run?
Up the backside of a jackrabbit
in less than a quarter mile
then turn for the sport,
and toss two coyotes
to the dirt.
But for all that,
my youth got buried
under a pile of life,
and I am left
with little more
than withering wit
to fend against
what fate has slated—
this fresh trouble
poised to trundle in.

Spinal Column

Hugh Burke

In the lowest strands
of a barbed wire fence
a spinal column hangs.

Bleak, sunseared and sharp.
Almost aglow. Its eerie calm,
the sediment of agony.

Witness to the verge.
Testament to solitary suffering.
State-of-the-art crucifixion.

Likely goat,
or, maybe a young deer. Either way,
a miserable end.

Still, the devout earth pulls,
wires stretch apart, and possibly
trailing souls may cross.

Mom's Feet

Shannon Golden

"You have mom's feet," he told me.

I looked down at them. I was barefoot on the cement patio. I was barefoot all summer. My feet were dry and coarse like the surface of a shortbread cookie. Like mom's, they were calloused farmer's feet, but that's not what Woody meant. My toes are small stubs, like plump little butterbeans. The nails are tiny caps on heads too big for them, just like mom's were.

"I reckon that's true." It's funny what you remember about people after they die.

He slouched in the webbed aluminum lawn chair that he always chose, under the fraying Phillies cap he always wore. I rocked on the cedar porch swing held by time-worn chains that groaned rhythmically in the sunset with each sway, like the throbbing aches in my hips at sunrise when I was picking vegetables.

"Thanks for helping me shell those peas." I was apologetic.

"No problem. Why did you plant so many?"

"Old habit, I guess."

He nodded. "Shelling peas reminds me of how mom would haul bucket after bucket down from the garden and dump them out on the picnic table. She'd have us kids sit there *all day* shelling peas into giant bowls. We would *shell* and *shell* and *shell* and that mound never shrunk. And the twins constantly fussing over who was going slower than the other one."

He retold the same stories the way old men do. I rocked and nodded in accompaniment.

Cricket song and darkness crept in around us. Citronella candles glowed. Drops of condensation from my iced tea glass dripped onto my belly and spread across my t-shirt when I drank. Time passed in silence and comfort.

"Welp, that's it for me, sis. I'm calling it a night. Thanks for supper." As he passed by, he reached his hand out for mine, offering a slip of a squeeze. A brush of palms like it had always been over the years. Never a hug, but the knowing touch of hands.

When he slid into his rusty white on red two-tone Silverado, I noticed duct tape binding the side view mirror. If only I had a dollar for every time I heard him say, "But she's a classic!" He ground the gears and reversed into the lawn, then chugged forward down the gravel drive. I raised my arm, hand upward, fingers spread in farewell, and I knew he was gesturing in a similar way out the open window of the truck, although we couldn't really see each other.

I went inside through the squeak and slam of the screen door. Upstairs, I perched on the edge of the tub to wash my feet. I admired them with a fresh eye, smoothing lotion into all the cracks and scuffs; soothing the butterbeans and arthritic knobs before bed.

I have mom's feet. And now mom's cancer. I didn't have the heart to tell Woody tonight. All our lives it's been the two of us, together through everything. The twins had each other. He and I were their babysitters, their adorers, their pallbearers. I thought I escaped the curse that took them all, but there I was, trying to figure out if I wanted to grapple with treatment like the twins or go quietly like mom. Trying to figure out if either option makes any kind of difference to stage IV.

In that moment, the surge of sadness was not for myself, but for my brother eventually alone in the world, no one left to share stories with on a lonely summer evening on the back porch.

I leaned in to regard my reflection in the bathroom mirror. Thinning graying hair loose from its daytime barrette. Grooves across my forehead. Eyes framed in a weathered face. Dad's face. Dad's eyes, nose, chin. My teeth crooked in all the same places as his. But I have mom's feet, worn and sturdy, that stand bare in wet muddy furrows of the garden. Feet that rock the porch swing after supper. Flesh and bone, reminders shared affectionately between siblings of a mother long gone.

I slid into bed.

Maybe I will tell him about the cancer tomorrow. Maybe I won't tell him at all. It's hard to know which choice is less cruel.

With March Comes Coyotes

Mark MacAllister

I heard them last night
at the mouth of the driveway
likely a bonded pair and their pups

they appear every spring
dependable as daffodils
just as the new families
in the ridiculous new houses
decide it's finally warm enough
to allow their cockapoos and ornamental chickens
unsupervised time in the back yard

our acres and those of our neighbors
form a safe corridor into what had been
until recently humid pine forest
tobacco barns   weedy two-tracks
deep fast creeks and more birds
       than one might count

over the coming weeks we'll keep to ourselves
not comment on posts
about the rhinestone collar
found still clasped in a cul-de-sac

some time ago they sent my cat home
with just a warning and a chunk
torn out of his left hind leg

now he spends his evenings on the porch
still startles when the lot of them gathers
ashamed and ecstatic
to share news of what they had no choice
       but to do

Big River

Claire Thomas

It was mid-July and Big Bend National Park stretched out before me, hot and wide. The sienna-colored peaks and gorges underscored variants of beige, and specks of green brush speckled the landscape like fireflies. For the few signs that appeared, my car, a salvaged sedan with extensive hail damage, obediently followed. The thermostat read 108 degrees. Although I was usually thankful for my car being black, as this partially obscured its craters, it was a rolling oven in the heat. It was also going on month five of having a busted air conditioner. One wrong turn, I thought, and my body would be found months later, having left the car in search of water, bones sun bleached like white desert calcite.

I eventually reached the parking lot. Empty, except for a single pickup truck. Either the eastern part of Big Bend was rarely explored or most people decided to spend their day without risking heat stroke. Walking across the asphalt lot toward the small Border Patrol building, I went with the latter. The Border Patrol agent couldn't have been older than 25, legs up on the desk, scrolling on his phone. Clearly not expecting anyone today, he straightened quickly upon hearing the door latch click shut. "Hi", I announce. "I'm looking to cross into Boquillas del Carmen, is this the right place?" "Yup", he nods. "This would be the place".

For context, my ability to locate trailheads was, and still is, equivalent to locating Malaysia Flight 370. If given the choice, I would walk straight into a random, thick wall of forest before I would ever take the time to pinpoint 40°25'18" N, 119°60'12" W. Therefore, I had preemptively researched Big Bend. I discovered that there was a post in the far eastern part of the park that allowed crossing over the Rio Grande into a small Mexican village named Boquillas del Carmen and I decided that would be my destination. Plus, no coordinates, no trailheads, no need to work yourself into a panic if you get lost. Just sit tight. Federal agents will come.

The border Patrol agent searched my backpack, glanced at my passport, and waved me toward the side door. "Out those doors, you will follow a short trail which takes you down to the riverbank. Once across the river, Boquillas sits about a half mile down the path. You'll have to be back by the time the patrol office closes, which is 6 pm." He glanced toward the clock, "so you have three hours." I set out on the mini trail, kicking up dried clay and dust. Droopy cottonwoods lined the way, providing relief from the unforgiving Texas noon and the sunlight that managed to sneak through dappled across my face.

At this part of the border, the Rio Grande was more like the Rio No Tan Grande, or Not So Big River. It was surprisingly narrow, its milky brown water slow and shallow. Across the Rio were approximately twenty Mexican men varying in age from late-teens to mid-seventies and they were looking at me. I waved somewhat self-consciously and one of the men, mid-sixties, heaved his rowboat off the bank and began to row over. Although I was underwhelmed by the river's size, its designation as a natural borderline was deserved. This stretch of the Rio Grande was just wild and unknowable enough to be impenetrable; a physical, literal boundary. Without a boat, at least.

My personal captain's skin was leathery, hands ashen and calloused as he rowed us back toward his side of the river. After a few attempts at conversing, he must have realized I didn't know a lick of Spanish. "No Espagnol?" The sun was beaming down on us causing my forehead to sizzle. "No, lo siento". A female with a guilt complex, I did know how to say I'm sorry. We resigned to exchanging occasional smiles for the remainder of the crossing, murky water sloshing against the boat.

Less than two minutes later, I had reached the Mexican side of the Not So Big River and climbed the bank to where my male posse was waiting. I had read that the locals often gathered at the Boquillas del Carmen crossing, ready to offer big-eyed American tourists horse rides or donkey escorts into town. The full experience, minus sombreros and a lingering mariachi band. A few men took turns presenting their donkeys and horses, some old, some matted, some bucking. The other men stood nearby shooting looks of uncertainty in my direction, clearly unaccustomed to visitors of the solo female variety.

I chose to ride a copper-colored horse and paid the owner ten dollars. The owner was an older man who looked even more sundried than my riverboat captain. He helped hoist me up into the saddle and introduced us, "This es Pinto". I took Pinto's reins in my hands. The owner, whose name I later learned was Sal, began motioning in the direction of town. I had neglected to mention that I did not know how to ride a horse, figuring it couldn't be too difficult; a little kick here, a slight pull on the reins there, the agreeable horse trotting along. That's not how it went, of course. Pinto began to squirm at the first tug and, before too long, was stomping in little agitated circles. "You know to ride?" Sal asked me. Bouncing around the saddle, Pinto's trots growing more heavy footed, I considered throwing myself off the straw-haired people-stomper. "Si" I answered. Then, linking my reins to his, Sal led me into town.

We sauntered toward Boquillas del Carmen, Pinto matching the wobble of Sal's horse up front. The ride was silent. Either Sal's English was limited to horseback riding terms or he was too busy considering ways he could make money that didn't include accommodating American tourists. The air was hot and still and smelled of mesquite. Hooves clacked in rhythm, as if adhering to an unseen metronome, as we passed beneath fig tree groves and along meadows of brittle desert grass. Once at the edge of town, I followed Sal's lead and dismounted, albeit gracelessly, and joined him in tying up the horses to a nearby post. Sal motioned toward a hill and I began my climb into town. Halfway up, I glanced behind me and saw that Sal was following me. I smile at him. Answering my unasked question, Sal says "I stay close".

At the crest of the hill sat a restaurant named Jose Falcon's. It was a stone building and I could hear Ranchera music escape from behind its doors, riding the hot breeze like an ice cream truck jingle in late July. I walked in and was promptly seated on the patio next to the only other patrons, an elderly couple drinking Jarritos and tapping their feet along to a two-man band. I ordered a margarita on the rocks, no salt, and enjoyed my first still moment of the day. The patio overlooked a rocky landscape. Not of the natural sort. Jagged cement blocks toppled over one another, bricks sprinkled throughout like confetti, and rusted pipes jutted up like weeds escaping through sidewalk cracks. A dilapidation medley. The band continued their serenade and I drank my gringorita, tapping along.

The village of Boquillas del Carmen was small and shaped in an oval. I walked down the dusty road with Sal following from a comfortable distance. A look of either concern or confusion tightened his face as I exited the restaurant and turned left instead of heading straight for the horses. Up the road, an open sign indicated a small store and I walked in. An old refrigerator kept RC cola cans and bottled water chilled. After a few minutes, I realized no one was coming so I set a dollar bill on the counter and left with my ice cold RC cola in hand. The village seemed to be home to no one as I continued down the road, houses falling to ruin along both sides. Like a ghost town after an earthquake. As the road turned and began its bend back toward the center, I heard laughter. Up ahead of me, two small girls were playing, mud caked up to their knees. The smaller of the two ran up to me as I passed. "Hola" she said, smiling through her missing baby teeth.

Not far ahead, an elderly man sat at a folding table that displayed his crafts for sale. An AM radio crackled from inside his house and an extension cord snaked up to the table, powering an old fan. On display were various animals made out of twisted and contorted copper wire and accented with colored beads. A coyote, a lizard, a sassy peacock. He smiled up at me, big and cheery, not giving a damn that he was missing far more teeth than the little girl making mud castles.Smiling back at him, I picked up the copper wire scorpion and made my purchase.

The tinkle of Jose Falcon's loyal entertainers came into range as I finished my town lap. I turned around to find Sal crunching along behind me, motioned toward the horses, and we slunk back toward the river. I had many miles left to travel that day via horse, boat, and hot car but I put it out of my mind. Come dusk, I would once again be tucked away in the high desert foothills of Texas, on the other side of the Not So Big River, drifting to sleep to ranchero music rolling across the plains.

Roadside Zoo

Mark MacAllister

Five dollars into an honor jar
admitted me to a gravel walkway
between rows of chickenwire boxes on sawhorses

labeled with index cards and occupied
by dull local snakes and lizards
turtles   possum and raccoon   one per cage
a waterbowl and some rubber toys for each

it was mid-afternoon South Carolina
so all dozed as designed

though disquieting I have witnessed schoolchildren
in more dire surroundings

at the far end a fancy felt letter sign behind glass
wolf it said   not gray wolf   Mexican wolf
red wolf or timber wolf   just *wolf*
and behind that a canid panting
          in blue tarpaulin shade

I know wolves well   he possessed none of the legginess
none of the long thin muzzle and gumline
the kinesis or that fear passed down

a husky/shepherd cross at best
perhaps some coyote seed snuck in there
back a generation or two

when I spoke to him with my voice
          climbed up
Hello there sweet boy
his tail gave him away

to be human is to hold opposing thoughts at once

and I found him to be both fraudulent and fetching

which then allowed me to accept that a dog
can certainly believe himself wolf (when of course he cannot)

which in turn reminded me that
        the planet's children
are so cherished and so entirely expendable

Appaloosa

Charles Gammon

Swirls all through the trance of gray clouds in their march above the
        day's last rider.
Full speed on a horse is bending the knee
to pulls in all directions;
and by pure luck,
strained muscles and soggy vision
happen to make a worthy trade in the agreement between us and them.

Our body is usually a sleuthy one,
and soon enough, reckoning precedes rejoicing
at the match of thigh to ribs with running
living angels;

truly, whichever ancients sway you,
a horse was there
and now with a dim silver halo like a crescent moon on its feet,
gives us something almost religious
when eating the carrots and celery from our palm while outlasting the
        gods.

As a child I remember
a drive to the coast, in the car after hours of
anointed blessings - American landscape
lining the sides of roads and highways.
Eventually, heaven answers a prayer, and without warning,

you pass a stretch of farmland with a corral holding horses
emerging orderly and beautiful enough to have been planted from the
        Earth
just moments before your eyes found them through the glass of the
        window.

Planespotting

Mike Herndon

Calvin awoke, as he did every morning, to the beeping of the coffee pot. It was a simple pleasure for the first thing he smelled each day to be the brewing of arabica beans. In recent weeks, he'd taken to sleeping on the couch in the living room, separated from the kitchen by only an island, and programming the pot to brew at seven. This way, he saved himself a few steps each morning and eliminated the need for an alarm clock.

He sat up, rotated himself, and sank his feet into the slippers he'd stepped out of eight hours before. The arthritis in his knees renewed his acquaintance as he stood. In the kitchen, he poured from the pot into the mug waiting on the counter, stirring in a spot of honey that he didn't really want. The older he got, the less sweetener he seemed to need. He ran some water in the kitchen sink, splashing his face and wiping his hands on the legs of his gray pajamas. The sliding glass door squeaked as he opened it to carry his coffee onto the deck, and he took a long, satisfying sip as he settled into his patio chair and waited for the 8:05 to taxi across the tarmac.

It had seemed a drawback, at first, to build so close to the airport, to have your island lifestyle adulterated by jet noise and your view dominated by a strip of concrete. But the land was cheaper on this side of the island, particularly if you wanted any elevation. There were only six flights a day – three inbound and three outbound – and while the noise bothered Ginny at first, they both grew accustomed to it. It was like living near the railroad tracks back in Ohio. After a while, it became background noise.

In St. Thomas, there were no trains and no snow and no HOAs and no morning commute. They'd moved here to escape all that, to build their dream house on the hill and enjoy retirement. St. Thomas had some of the best views in the Caribbean, and as an American territory it was easy to move here without severing ties to the mainland.

The house looked like a one-story structure from the road, built of concrete like most of the rest of the homes on the island. But a view from the water would have revealed two stories, with the second built into the side of the mountain below. The plans included three bedrooms, two baths, a well-appointed kitchen and a spacious office. Solar panels on the roof helped energy costs, and there were garden boxes in the terraced backyard where they grew their own tomatoes, cucumbers and herbs. Wide decks extended off both floors, affording them a view of the sunset over the water, as well as all the takeoffs and landings at Cyril King Airport.

They were annoying at first, but they came to look forward to them. The planes marked their days, from the first takeoff at 8:05 in the morning until the last arrival at 4:25 in the afternoon. They were noisy reminders that the world continued spinning beneath their lounge chairs. From their morning coffee to their afternoon mojitos and margaritas, they watched the population of the island fluctuate, 150 passengers at a time.

For what seemed like the hundredth time that day, David hoisted the nets up from the back of the boat. His T-shirt was soaked with sweat and the seawater that splashed over the gunnel, and he struggled to keep his footing on a deck turned slick by fish guts. Surely, he thought, there were more enjoyable ways to spend a day on the water.

He saw the sport-fishing boats careening past, their shiny dual 300s purring like two dozen sleeping kittens, and wondered what it must be like to do this for fun, to not feel defeated if he returned with less than the limit. But there was no sense, he reminded himself, in comparing his life to theirs. Besides, it was the last haul of the day. It was time to head in.

The upside to working a fishing boat in St. Thomas is that the season is almost year-round. The downside is that while it pays more than cleaning hotel rooms, schlepping drinks or hawking jewelry on the beach, it still wasn't enough to get you far living here. Then the pandemic found its way to the island and the work evaporated overnight. Most of the restaurants closed, leaving no market for the fish they caught. Waiters and hotel workers found themselves working odd jobs or panhandling in the streets. Deckhands were kept busy for a while, especially those handy enough to help out with refits, but most of the boats eventually went into dry dock and they joined the ranks of the unemployed.

St. Thomas depended on tourists for survival. He could never remember a time when he didn't see them wandering through the streets in their brightly colored shorts and flip flops, drinking banana daquiris and snapping photographs. The boats were larger now, the cameras had become cellphones and the tourists took more photos of themselves than the scenery around them.

He was out of work nearly two years, but thankfully vaccines were developed and the tourists returned, pouring out of their cruise ships. They were fantastically massive, like floating cities with water slides sprouting off their decks, and when two of the bigger ones were docked at both Havensight and Crown Bay they nearly doubled the population of Charlotte Amalie.

Slowly the restaurants and hotels reopened. The fishing boats returned to the water. The men and women who caught the fish, those who cooked it and those who served it were put back to work. Some chose to remain unemployed, having taken to life on the streets or alternate means of income, but David returned to the boats as soon as they hit the water. He'd worked them since he was a boy and, while the days were long and hot and the work was hard, he had come to enjoy it. It kept his mind busy. There was something about being on a boat that felt liberating, even when you are rooted to the same spot on the deck for ten hours, lowering and hoisting nets until the sky fades from blue to orange and red and shades of purple.

If he didn't love it, he wouldn't have come back. He hadn't been idle in his unemployment. He'd fallen into something lucrative enough that fishing was now his second income. So maybe he knew a little of how those sport fishermen felt after all.

The 8:05 was an American Airlines 727, sleek and shiny, which lifted skyward with a delayed roar. Calvin used got up to use the restroom and refill his coffee mug before watching the 9:30, a Delta A300, touch down neatly in an almost perfect landing. Cyril King's 7,000-foot runway is too short for the bigger 747s and A320s, but it's more than enough room for the narrow-body jets, leaving heavy braking largely unnecessary. Watching through the binoculars, Calvin saw a slight hop on initial touchdown, leaving this flight's landing just short of the best he'd ever seen on the island.

It had been a weekday two years ago, a sunny June morning with the azure sky fading into the deeper blue of the water, white wisps of clouds floating just above the horizon. It was the 2:15 arrival, if he remembered correctly. The Delta A300 descended as though lowered by a giant hand, settling softly onto the runway without pause. Looking through the binoculars, it didn't even seem like the tires compressed as they touched the pavement. It was one fluid motion, from airborne to landing to taxiing to fully stopped at the gate.

"Wow," Ginny said. "Won't see one better than that."

She was right. A week later, she was gone. The stroke had come out of nowhere. She'd never even had high blood pressure. It couldn't have taken Calvin more than a few minutes to recognize the slurred speech and the sagging in her face, but it took the ambulance a half-hour to reach them, and by the time they got her to the hospital it was too late. He held her limp hand as he watched the light fade from her eyes. Her will and her wishes had always been clear: She did not want to be kept alive artificially by machines.

The Delta departure took off uneventfully at 11:45, powering gracefully skyward. A new planeload of visitors would replace it in a few hours. He imagined what it'd be like to see this place for the first time, to marvel at the too-blue water, to take in the view from the hillsides with virgin eyes. And how would it then feel to leave again, newly tanned and rested, heading back home to your family, your job, your life? He drained the dregs of his coffee and went inside, as the heat would soon become oppressive.

He set the mug in the sink and rubbed his bald head. It still felt strange to him, all these years later, to find no hair there. He turned both knobs and washed his hands, frowning as the water failed to turn warm. Opening a drawer in the island, he retrieved a lighter and crossed the room to open the door to the stairwell. His knees creaked as he made his way down the rough two-by-sixes to what he now considered the basement, with its dirt floor and cinder block walls. Open doorways led to other unfinished rooms. In one of them, surrounded by discarded furniture, stood the hot water heater.

He knelt in the sandy dirt and looked beneath it. After struggling for a time with the uncooperative lighter, he relit the pilot light, groaning as he grabbed onto the back of a padded chair and the edge of the old dining room table and lifted himself back upright. Light flooded the room from the uncovered window, particles of dust floating over the table and chairs and bedframes and chests of drawers like tiny, useless snowflakes as he turned and trudged back upstairs.

The Charlotte Rose docked quietly, like a key slipped into a lock. Simmie, the other deckhand, helped David tie off the bow and stern ropes. When the boat was secure, they began unloading the hold. It wasn't full, but not a bad haul.

Mickey, the captain, climbed down from the wheelhouse and sat on the bottom step, sipping coffee and watching them work. Damn near eight years David had worked for this man and he never remembered seeing him lift a finger in dock. But he didn't push as hard as some other captains he'd seen and he didn't cuss them too much, so he was all right.

With the hold was emptied, David and Simmie collected their money for the day and trudged to their respective vehicles in the lot. Two dogs nosed around the tires of David's pickup and he shooed them away, opening the creaky door and sliding inside. Damn dogs roamed the whole island. Some were strays, some probably rabid, but others had collars and were obviously pets let loose to wander. It wasn't their fault their owners were such assholes, he thought, but he hated them just the same. The truck finally rattled to life after several turns of the key, and he made a mental note of looking for a battery that might fit it the next time he did a job, however unlikely that might be.

It hadn't been just the restaurants and hotels that were empty during the pandemic, but the summer homes too – those McMansions dotting the shoreline and the hillsides where wealthy people from Miami and Jacksonville came to vacation a month or two each year. They flew in instead of coming by boat but air travel also dried up overnight, leaving only a handful making their annual trek by private plane while the rest of the houses on the hillsides stood vacant. For an enterprising young man like himself, those represented opportunities.

Most of the houses had alarm systems, but he found that many had been disabled. Even the wealthy were looking for ways to save a buck. He carried his pistol just in case, a Glock he'd found in an upstairs closet of the first house he ever hit, and usually brought a bottle of

Cruzan. One was to give himself the courage to go in. The other, if necessary, was to get himself out.

As time went by, he found he didn't need either, but he carried them out of habit. On the rare occasion that he tripped an alarm, getting out before the police service arrived was never a problem. Timely response wasn't one of their strengths. And after the first few houses, he found that he no longer harbored whatever moral or logistical reservations he'd once had about the process. There was a very low probability of getting caught, and the people from whom he was stealing were wealthy enough to replace whatever he took. It was no more than an inconvenience to them.

He found this irritating, so he began to seek out ways to make their loss more meaningful. He kicked holes in the walls or pried up kitchen tiles. He ripped off door and cabinet handles. He disconnected shower heads and wall outlets. If time did not become an issue, he'd trash the place like a rock star's motel room. Who were they to live in such luxury while the majority of the rest of the island lived hand to mouth? What had they done to deserve it? Had they ever pulled a twelve-hour day on a fishing boat? Had they ever felt real pain?

As with most days on the boat, loading up was easy, but the unloading proved a greater challenge. It took a couple months to find an antiques dealer with some vision who knew that exporting could be just as lucrative as importing. He'd taken all he could carry from his earliest jobs, piling it ceiling-high in his garage, but the dealer seemed interested only in the artwork and any furniture that had been light enough for him to wrangle onto the truck by himself. So he'd recruited his cousin Lenny and soon they were hauling out dressers, bureaus and even armoires, packed up and ready to be sent off for resale in Miami.

Over the two years that represented the height of the pandemic, he'd managed to make enough money to get a larger apartment and Lenny had been able to move out of his parents' house. When the vaccines beat back the virus and the summer residents returned to their burgled homes in the hills, their furniture and artwork were already safely in Florida, most of the money already spent. They filed police reports, but those crimes were by now ancient history. The cops didn't even bother.

It was hot for a while, and they shut it down while the cops ramped up patrols through the hills. David returned to the boats, and Lenny went back to running his beach chair and umbrella business, but they weren't going to stop. The money was too good. They'd need to be more selective in their targets with the homeowners back on the island. But once things died down, they'd be right back at it.

Calvin pulled a loaf of bread from the pantry and a bag of turkey, a head of lettuce and some mustard from the refrigerator. Laying his ingredients on the counter, he set about making his lunch. He poured a glass of tea and took his sandwich to the couch that doubled as his bed. From there, he could see the TV mounted to the wall, but he did not turn it on. Below it was a table with framed photographs that he no longer looked at but couldn't bring himself to throw away. The rest of the room was bare.

They'd designed the house with this open concept with entertaining in mind. While he was pouring drinks in the kitchen, Ginny could be chatting with their guests in the living room and they'd still all be together, in the same space, not separated by walls. But they'd never made many friends here. They hadn't gone out as much as she'd hoped, as he'd been content to sit in the little paradise they'd made and watch the jets land and the sun set. He took a bite of the sandwich and stared out the window to the water beyond the airport. The day looked bright and hot and the water bluer than blue, contrasting sharply with the white walls around him.

Around those walls were closed doors, behind which lay mostly empty rooms. They'd delayed completing the house when money grew tight, and there was little point now. After Ginny died, he began selling off the contents of the rooms he no longer used, or tossing them downstairs. Their bed was the first thing to go. He hadn't slept in it since her death and couldn't imagine ever sliding between its sheets again. He hadn't washed them since that terrible day, but her scent faded like everything else, and he threw them out with the trash.

This house was no longer home, it was just a place where he stayed. It was supposed to be their dream home. Now all he could think about was how badly he wanted to leave. The planes reminded him every day. But where would he go? Ohio? Some other place? How would it be any different? It was too much to think about, so he drank his coffee and watched other people come and go.

After his lunch, he showered and threw on a fresh T-shirt and pair of shorts for the drive into town. Since he'd been so reluctant to go anywhere when Ginny was still here, it seemed the least he could do now. The Jeep cranked right up despite its advancing age and carried him down Crown Mountain Road in less than ten minutes, leaving him wondering yet again why it had taken the ambulance so long.

He sat outside a bistro in the Old Town, staring across the bay at Hassel Island and drinking a Bud Light. He'd never developed a taste for the local beers. Tourists walked up and down the promenade in front of him. Sunbathers reclined in lounge chairs on a small strip of beach overlooking the bay, waving off the entrepreneurs offering them bracelets and straw hats. Enterprising young men called out to passersby, looking to fill more lounge chairs. "If it ain't Lenny," one called, "you don't want any."

Among the throng was a man oppressively dressed in blue jeans and a waistcoat in the June heat. Calvin hadn't noticed him at first, much like the others on the promenade who passed him by on either side without a glance. He finished beer and motioned to the waitress for another as he continued to watch the man. And as he stared he came to realize that ever so slowly, almost imperceptibly, the man was walking. Backward.

He took a step backward and stopped, holding his place as tourists walked to either side of him. Then he took another step. And stopped. And waited. Wherever he was going, he didn't seem to be in much of a hurry.

"He's out here just about every day," the waitress said as she set his beer on the table. "Tonight, he'll be walking backward the other way."

"Why?" Calvin asked.

"Who knows?" she said. "Crazy. Confused. Bored. Why does anyone do anything?"

It was a good question, he thought after she left him with his beer. As the man in front of him took another slow, deliberate step backward, he had no answer for it.

Four hours later, Calvin stood from the table and nearly fell over. He'd found sitting and drinking near the water even more enjoyable than sitting on his deck, but as the sky darkened and the streetlamps illuminated, he realized it was getting late. He'd switched from beer to liquor upon seeing the bistro's prodigious bourbon selection, and it had gone down smoothly. He didn't realize how drunk he was until he stood up.

He grabbed hold of the table to steady himself, looking around quickly to assure himself that no one had noticed. It was a short drive home, but all he could think of was how humiliating it would be to see blue lights in his rearview mirror. The weather was beautiful, and the liquor had left him feeling warm and invigorated, if a bit unsteady. He decided it was a nice night for a walk.

He crossed the street and walked up the promenade, crossing another street to begin the ascent uphill. Traffic was light and he barely broke stride at either of the crossings. He found himself winded quickly as he got to the steeper part of the hill, however, and he stopped frequently to catch his breath. Each time he stopped, it took longer to start again, as the pain that seemed a memory in his drunkenness now grabbed hold of his knees and reminded him of its presence.

It was during his third such hiatus that he saw the figure approaching him. He couldn't make out its features in the dim light of dusk, but as it neared he saw the backside of the waistcoat and blue jeans he'd noticed earlier at the bistro. It was Backwards Man, but he was no longer moving slowly. His legs were pumping like pistons, in fluid motion, and he was approaching so quickly Calvin watched him carefully to make sure his eyes weren't deceiving him. He seemed to be running downhill as though facing forward. He watched the back of the man's head as it neared, half-expecting to see eyes, nose and a mouth but seeing instead only the nape of his neck.

"What?" Calvin started to ask but the man high-stepped backward past him, all knees and elbows, and disappeared around a bend in the road before the question could be completed. He'd seemed determined leave wherever he'd been as quickly as he could, while not being able to turn his eyes from it. Or maybe he just didn't care to see where he was going. Calvin stared at the space the man had stepped backward through, the edge of the roadway now eerily still. He'd never seen the man's face, and now it was as though he'd never been there at all.

Calvin turned and continued trudging uphill. When he reached his house, he stumbled inside and pulled the bourbon from a cabinet, pouring himself a glass and falling into his favorite chair on the deck to watch the day end. The sky seemed stratified, with the grays and blacks of the emerging night streaked with a bedrock of pinks and purples. It was at this time of day that he felt her presence, sitting there beside him in her chair. They'd always enjoyed these times in silence, content to just be while the sun dipped around the edge of the world for another round. It had taken effort not to try to fill that silence with something – a laugh, a joke, anything. But it felt like a gift now, because all he had to do was be quiet and stare into the fading hues of the dying day to feel her beside him again, enjoying it with him.

Eventually darkness took over and she was gone again, an empty chair. And here, after the best time of his day, came the worst. He felt her loss again every night. Everything ends badly, he thought. Empires fall. Buildings rot and collapse. Cars break down and sit rusting in junkyards. Money dwindles away, stolen or wasted. Bones turn brittle, hearts weaken and minds grow fuzzy. Love fades into meaninglessness, explodes in jealousy and deceit, or just dies.

His own end would be no different. He felt it closer every day. At times, he wished it would go ahead and get here already, to end the insufferable dread of its approach. He stood and leaned over the railing, peering into the darkness of the trees and brush and the weeds that had overtaken his neglected garden boxes two stories below. It'd be easy, a simple matter of gravity.

But he'd been drinking. Better to sleep it off and sober up. The darkness would still be there tomorrow night.

There was an alarm company's sign in the yard but no signs of a system installed. Lots of people just put a sign out to try to fool you into thinking there was one. There was no car in the driveway and no lights on anywhere on the property. The shrubbery was a bit overgrown and the grass in the small front yard was high, but the construction and style of the house was a giveaway that there was money inside. Maybe not as much as the other side of the island, but any hillside was prime real estate. David and Lenny slipped in through the front door, its single lock easily defeated, and immediately felt betrayed by their assumptions. The house looked nearly empty. There was a nice TV, but those were a dime a dozen. A nondescript couch. Not much else.

This was just his damn luck, he thought. He hadn't had a good haul in weeks. It was getting harder and harder to find unoccupied houses, as the island repopulated. And now, when he'd found what seemed like a perfect target, it held nothing of value. He wondered again whether he was cursed.

It was a feeling he'd had often in the last few years, since Freddie's death. Why else would he have been taken so early, a child? What possible explanation for it could there be, unless a punishment? He hadn't been around enough, hadn't given enough of himself, hadn't loved deeply enough. He took a swig of Cruzan as he looked at the cabinets and wondered how quickly he could dismantle them. These people would feel the pain he felt. The rum did nothing anymore. The only way to relieve it was to share it, to take it out on someone or something else.

But this house felt different somehow, and not just because it was largely empty. As he continued looking around at the few belongings in the expansive room, he began to understand why. Maybe the things that happened to those around you had nothing to do with you, he thought; maybe they had nothing to do with punishment or blame. Maybe shit just happened, some of it blissful and undeserved, some of it cruel and unfair.

"Hey man," he heard Lenny say after a time, "you okay?"

Just as he realized the wetness on his face was tears, he heard what sounded like a groan. He and Lenny stared at each other as he reached inside his jacket for the Glock. This house wasn't empty after all.

Calvin had been asleep when the world around him exploded. The walls, the ceiling, the very air shattered in ear-splitting sound. He heart pounded double-time as he sat up in an unfamiliar room and looked around the darkness. A thought crossed his mind and hovered there, crystalizing from fantasy to potential truth, prodding him to get up and test it, to try it on like a new pair of shoes and see if it felt right. But if it were true, if this was where he was going and not where he'd been, there was nothing he could do about it anyway. So he went back to sleep.

When he awoke again, he realized as the bright sun filtered through the blinds that he was in the guest bedroom. It was the one room he'd left fully furnished, on the off chance he ever had company that needed it, and he had to admit his body felt better after a night in an actual bed, even if his head did not. His mouth felt like sandpaper, and the jackhammer pounding inside his head dissipated only slightly as he stood and moved toward the door. Outside the room, the house looked much as he'd left it the evening before. The microwave clock told him it was nearly nine. He opened a cabinet and took out a glass, poured some water from the tap and drank it down one long gulp.

The coffee pot, however, was empty and turned off. He must have forgotten to fill and set it in his tipsy state the night before, but then he noticed other curiosities. His photo of Ginny stood on the counter, her smiling face surrounded by a wooden frame that read "In God's Hands." Beneath it was the appointment slip for his oncologist, which he thought he remembered sticking to the refrigerator with a magnet. Also on the counter was a bottle of rum, nearly full.

"I wish I could tell you about this morning," he said absently, looking out the window, where the bright sun shone down mercilessly on the slab of cement where his Jeep normally stood. Beyond it in the driveway, near the road, was what looked like an animal, a dog maybe, the pool of blood around it dried nearly black.

He started for the front door, but saw the time for hurrying had passed. Must have been hit by a car. He pulled the coffee and filters from the cabinet, but then put them back. What was the point now, he thought, as he made his way down the stairs to get his shovel. It was down there somewhere, among the old furniture and gardening tools in the dust. He'd already missed the 8:05 anyway.

Fish Story

Richard Band

My brother no longer goes to Stumpy Pond,
says his fishing buddies either passed away
or had their boats repossessed.
Same brother got behind
on his motorcycle payments
but he managed to wreck it
and insurance paid it off.

So I'm offering to give him a ride
to the river where he can fish
from the bank and I'm offering
to sit with him and have a beer,
and watch the line bob
and watch the ripples dance,
and he will tell tales about
the girls that got away.

I will listen and ponder
life's winds and waves,
and remember a time
I was casting about,
and the net held,
and she will likely buzz my phone
to say I hope you and Ben
are having a good time.

Iron Out

Hugh Burke

Folded tissues
embed the band of a straw hat
to keep it snug.

Stories spread
from a slender frame
gathered into the leather,
lampside chair.

Deep as dusk, his voice
replicates Cash's chorus
to make us laugh.

Crossword puzzles
rise from folded knees,
collect his words as rivers
collect the rain.

A swift kink to the neck
drops a nod on some stranger
who, smitten and esteeming,
nods right back.

His blade returns into itself;
having slipped each seam of wrapping,
the gift reveals.

Like the sloop's hard-earned headway,
his stride, between thin swaying hands,
consumes roiling pastures.

An old coffee can chimes against a bucket.
From the riverbottom, sheep

spill forth like waves
to enshroud him.

My Nephew the Body of Water

Marie Chambers

Every day I swim about a mile and a half. Not rapidly but constantly, I swim. I've done this for so long, for so many years, that I no longer need to spend much energy thinking about swimming itself. A lap to get accustomed to the water temperature. Another lap to make sure my lane partner is staying on his side. Then I am free to re-imagine the world. The ill will that most days invades my google feed prior to the morning swim gets laundered by the steady flow of energy in my body. The water resists me. It makes my forward motion difficult and in so doing demands that I devote myself only to forward motion. There is something in this equation that liberates me from worldly weight-bearing issues and enables me to problem solve all situations without any form of constraint.

Most days, I start with the breaststroke and keep my head above water. Ideas begin swimming with me.

My niece just had a baby. Weirdly enough his name is a body of water: River. I wonder how he's feeling about needing to evacuate the sweet warm waters of his mother and grapple with gravity and air and the feel of other people. I wonder if he likes his parents. I know they like him but getting that to be a mutual deal is hard to predict. There's no code of conduct that makes it real. Even in the safety of my daily swim, I have choices about stroke and tempo. It's frequently necessary to disregard the advice of other swimmers. What if River is a go-with-the-flow guy and his parents' parents keep suggesting that schedules make for happy babies. Lots of people want to weigh in. Everyone has a terrific idea and they really want everyone else to be terrifically happy so they tell you their idea over and over and over. Or they give you the most insightful book with all the tips you need for successful parenting. How in the world can anyone discover their intuitive understanding of any other person with all this advice? 'How to' my ass, I say to myself. More than 'how to' is *what*. What do I observe? What do I hear or see or smell or taste? What is this being in front of me? I don't think ye olde 'who' even registers until you have thoroughly investigated 'what.'

On a whim, my backstroke begins.

What will we do with all the parentless children being created while I form this sentence? In Gaza, the Ukraine, Syria, Somalia, Myanmar, even the US border with Mexico and on and on. What can these children become? Given the severity of their need, the seeming inaccessibility of assistance, how can they evolve into anything but a swarm of terrorists? Or a swarm of sheep who can be manipulated by singular terrorists. I suppose sheep don't innately swarm but a multitude traveling in one direction with no thought but survival acquires an unnatural force and that unnaturalness is what makes me think sheep might swarm.

Isn't that what happens in a war? Lots of plans. Tons of advice. Then some incursion tears through the somewhat thin veneer of civility and we are sheep or bees or water buffalo and we move as one to insure survival of everything else but the he or she who stands in the path of greatest jeopardy. Whatever the weapon being deployed, it is endlessly eternally the dearly beloved human who surrenders their life to the will and for the greater good of the swarm. Or the swarm leader.

What if River is just not a swarm kind of human? He wants to do a sidestroke in the fast lane and will not take up arms against anyone. Can his family find a way to love him as he is? Bigger picture here, can the larger family of fellow humans on this earth learn to love those whose 'as he is' is not to their liking?

I don't know that this conundrum is what my darling niece is contemplating now. She lives in the surreal post-partum world of exhaustion book-marked by the business of feeding, sleeping, burping, napping, dressing and undressing, washing the soiled onesies and making sure her little one keeps his mittens on so he doesn't scratch out his eyes by mistake or miscalculation. No doubt she is falling in love with him too. Despite every difficulty, her very being propels her towards love. I am swimming and dreaming on how we might learn to bear the horrors of the world without losing the hope of loving it despite the horror.

Maybe we are not so far apart after all.

My father reoccurs here. He's a slender, olive skinned, wavy-haired youth staring down the camera. He's perched near the gun of the tank he drove through Europe for General Patton in WWII. I found this picture when we cleaned out the file cabinets after he died. There he sits, on the verge, ready to fly, ready to do more driving. More something. I cannot read his eyes. I don't know where he is but I know he is not home. I know he has seen some terrible things. Some inhuman things. Yet I also know who he will become. I know who he will be for me. If this terrible combat marked him, and it must have, I cannot read it here in this ancient image I've conjured for some reason during lap 36 of this Wednesday's swim.

My lane partner decides to put on swim paddles. So there's a necessary pause at the shallow end where he's stashed the his swim bag and the aforementioned swim paddles.

I hate those bloody paddles. As if the American Crawl needs to be weaponized. Then I notice a rather larger red heart inked into his right shoulder and forgive him his paddles a little bit.

I don't have any tattoos but the idea of a tattoo as the only means of demonstrating how we have been marked by life pleases me. As in: the bird on my shoulder is for my mother who loved to sing; the small fish on my ankle is in honor of Samuel my cat who loved to eat tuna; knives for the second husband etc. Like that. I get that. Good on my lane partner for the heart.

The other scars, the marks that refuse to form visible scar tissue, those are the ones that hijack my days, interrupt my swim and send me shivering to the locker room. I imagine I'm not alone in my experience of this kind of panic.

However, I am lucky. I had, and to this day have, the north star certitude of my parents to safeguard the rest of the afternoon and then right on to the swim I know I will embark on tomorrow. I'm very lucky.

Kickboard. By my count, I've done the mile and now I do kickboard. My tempo is slow as mud and I curse the board but every day I do it.

Out the front window, the sky is blue as baby blankets. My lane partner surrenders the dread swim paddles and exits the water. Suddenly my lane is clear and still as an aqua sky. Different from a recognizably blue sky. Somehow, via the wonders of chlorine, the color seems equal parts magical and unreasonable. And my little body of water nephew floats back into my mind.

I hope River is lucky. I'm rooting for his new earthbound

family. I'm rooting for all the earth's earthbound families. I'm rooting for all of them everywhere.

What We Feed

Morrow Dowdle

It's not that I think women should be in the kitchen—
hell, no. But something happens when my daughter and I
watch a documentary in which Sardinian women
spend their days cooking. Kerchiefed, aproned,
many of them cresting a century in age, they stand
hours to shape pasta for minestrone, use ancient starter
to bake sourdough that actually lowers blood sugar.

We hold hands, tear up, swear we will visit
those terraced hills to find the ones who pour olive oil,
chop onions blade beside hand, careless of the men
lazing at café tables or playing bocce. We will learn
their alchemy, summon what calls them to spend hours
making what will be devoured in minutes.

My mother, always on simmer, boiled away like beans
that would not soften, but in the kitchen she would settle.
The clink of lid on pot, marinara fragrance meant
I could breathe, hear nothing of her but jazz albums,
her hum and whistle. Maybe a random *Goddammit!*
but the rage went on vacation. . . .

And a week after my latest breakdown,
I am in my kitchen mixing cornstarch and cocoa
for chocolate cream. It is Sunday afternoon.
I am alone, measured only by cup and spoon,
the gravity of what they carry. The children
and their father rest in bedrooms. Outside,

the sky is the stabilizing sort of blue that comes
when winter stumbles into spring. Vinyl spins
quiet, I stir as recipe suggests—continuous,
over heat—wait for it to thicken. No wonder

hearth contains the name—I am in the heart
of the house, I am its heart, its beat. It has so little
to do with what we cook, but what we feed.

See

Charles Gammon

Mid-April,
when the year's resurrections are moving closer to a pause,
and it takes so much for little miracles to happen at all,
I arrive at a simple place
a path to
a cheap, black metal table outside the restaurant.
Wind. Walk. Smile. Thank you. Sit.
Water with lemon.
A clear sky that was made to warm me.

Seeing, for myself now, how even the curve the body draws is drowned
        in kinds of shyness
when the sun kisses it with a clean wet mouth.

See, I am out of my mind
because I am empty, and only have so much to give to daydreams
but forfeit better efforts and waste them with plans of how to be more
        myself.
Because I see my shade spewed in black chalk on the concrete
as it peers back at me
and still want to swallow it.
an easy breeze to your skin before putting out the bonfire.

Legacy

Nancy Werking Poling

I have no photographs of my father laughing. The image I carry in my mind is one in which his eyelids droop, his jaw is firm, his lips jut out in a dejected pout.

I grew up believing his sadness was my fault.

I argued with him. I wanted to go to dances. No, dancing was a sin. I wanted to wear shorts. Florida days were hot and all the other girls did. No, displaying my body was a sin. I wanted to wear nail polish. No, that was a sin too.

To my youthful mind, my father spoke for God. Not the God of compassion, or the God of retribution, but the God of Ten-plus Commandments. Admonitions from God the Daddy left me confused about my body. If it must be covered, if I was not to draw attention to it, it must be inherently evil.

And the evil my body carried made Daddy sad.

My mother did what she could to ease his gloom. Evenings, after washing dinner dishes and putting them away, she would sit at the piano and play "Precious Lord, Take my Hand," "I Come to the Garden Alone," "Nearer My God to Thee." Seated in his easy chair, Daddy closed his eyes. A look of calm spread across his face.

As an adult I'm able to understand my father in ways my adolescent self could not. He was clinically depressed, but at the time no doctor diagnosed the problem. Was he depressed because his widowed mother forced him to farm the land she'd purchased and give up his dream of going to college? Did my mother, in the privacy of their bedroom, let him know he was inadequate? Did she insist that if he'd only try harder he could jolt himself out of his melancholy? Or did he carry a gene of sorrow, one that felt the world's hurt? I don't recall his mother, my grandmother, smiling either. No doubt my father would have done anything humanly possible not to feel the deep sorrow he carried.

Daddy left me no memories of fun or laughter. If I allow myself to recall ordinary times, though, I recognize one gift as valuable, perhaps more valuable, than laughter.

Our house was built of concrete block, with a galley kitchen and a miniscule dining room. Our furniture was worn. But we had something I never saw in friends' homes. We had two sets of encyclopedias: *The Encyclopedia Britannica,* and *World Book,* both purchased on monthly payment plans. I spent hours thumbing through *World Book,* fascinated by pictures and diagrams on subjects ranging from Automobile to Zodiac. What makes a car engine turn the wheels? I asked. Why do fingernails keep growing after I've cut them off? Why did John Wilkes Booth assassinate Abraham Lincoln? Whatever happened to the Seminole Indians? Daddy would get out an encyclopedia. Together we searched for answers. In retrospect I see his reverence for knowledge, his willingness to encourage my curiosity.

Mom must have had her fill of his sadness. She filed for divorce after I graduated from college. Daddy took off for Washington State, as far as he could get from Florida and still be on the mainland United States.

I was inaccessible by phone when he died alone, far from family. My husband, our children, and I had been camping in Vermont. Upon our return home I got a call saying that Daddy had taken his own life. Inside a garage he attached a hose to the tailpipe of his car. By the time I received the message, my brother had arranged for the body to be shipped to Indiana, where our ancestors are buried.

Peering inside the open casket, I saw a familiar expression on my father's face: the scowl of the deep sadness he carried. "Precious Lord, take my hand," I imagine him thinking toward the end. "I am tired; I am weak; I am worn."

I wanted fun and laughter. Daddy bequeathed to me a love of knowledge.

The Single Life

Karen Luke Jackson

It wasn't your choice the day he vacated
the family home, briefcase in one hand,
hangered suits in the other. Or perhaps it was

your refusal to ignore the chair he heaved
across the room, the fist he slammed into a wall
because you'd confronted his newest love interest.

And there's his side: how remodeling the house
wrecked his credit, how you got a promotion
and didn't *stand by your man* when he lost his job.

Three sessions in, the counselor
concludes: *you've grown too far apart.*
As if you didn't know.

Married friends promise: *We're here for you both.*
Men golf with him, now their guest. Women lunch
with you, avoiding chatter about charity events,

shopping trips, the trek to Machu Picchu when
you were still married. Memories strewn
with egg shells and land mines. A few pull

you to the side, tell you how lucky
you are: *you can do anything
you want, anywhere, anytime.*

Soon excuses roll like movie credits:
*Started a new diet. Have to work
this weekend. Entertaining guests.*

You meet other women—divorcees, widows,
never married. They warn: *it's a couples' world.*
Tax breaks. Health care. Two for the price of one.

One morning, at a new coffee shop,
a latte steaming in your hand,
you run into one of your old friends.

She fumbles for words: *Heard you'd moved*
away. I never left, you say and turn
toward the door.

Sitting in My Sister's Living Room: A Miracle

Morrow Dowdle

Her dog has been diagnosed with cancer.
It manifests, suddenly, as brain-shaped tumor
at his gumline, dime-sized. The pendulous
pink bit peeks from the corner of his lip.

The smell of it divulges rotting meat,
stepping already over death's brink.
Still, he trots chipper to his bowl, gobbles
attention from all willing fingers.

How late we apprehended the stink
of our own malignance. How we waited
for each other to change while our cells
mutated in secret. But we have made

our admissions, emptied ourselves of apology.
If ever I was jealous of her wealth, her friends,
I no longer cross that threshold. This home
simple now, few blessed to enter.

The dog will die in hours, our father dead
much longer—he, our deepest sickness.
And yet, we mend. Our talks like rounds
of radiation, the singe fresh on our lips.

We stay up late into the night. Knowing
we'll feel miserable the next day, we do it
anyway. The dog curls on a pillow.
We sit vigil. We make medicine of this.

Soldier's Salute

Carol Luther

Word came that Matthew Hawkins had gone missing, and he'd taken his father's rifle with him.

It was a Saturday, and I was sitting in the dining room of the Lintz Hotel, finishing a slice of Miss Marnie's delectable apple cobbler that always had just the right touch of cinnamon to it, when I saw the commotion in the lobby through the door of the dining room. Two men were questioning Miss Maisie, Miss Marnie's twin, who was tending the reception on what was usually a slow afternoon.

One of the men went upstairs, and the other stepped into the dining room and scanned the tables. He spotted lumber company people in the corner, finishing up their coffee and chewing over the latest war news from Europe and from the Pacific. He went over to speak with the lumber men and then hurried out. The lumber men had some conversation, and then they hustled out also.

I finished the cobbler sooner than usual and went straight to Miss Maisie to ask, and she told me the news. "Well, Miss Neville, Matthew said something about looking for early blackberries, his mama said, and she was so glad he was getting out of the house that she didn't think anything of it." Miss Maisie breathlessly continued--almost any excitement tended to bring that on--that after his mama started gathering some wash off the line and bringing it in to sort, she saw that the door to the little closet under the stairs was just barely open, and they always kept it locked because that's where the guns were. She looked in and saw right away that the rifle was missing, and it like to have given her the palpitations because she was worried about Matthew ever since he'd come home from the war with the half-healed burns over his face and left arm, refusing to see anybody or anything. He'd have to go back for more surgery, poor thing, and he'd dreaded it. He was so self-conscious he didn't want to see anybody, not even any of his high school friends who were still around.

I remembered Matthew and the boys he ran around with in high school. They'd been in my drawing class. I'd come to Settico Plains, Tennessee, several years ago to paint a mural in the post office for the WPA and had stayed to teach in the high school and sketch and paint in the Great Smoky Mountains.

His mama, Miss Maisie continued, didn't know what was going to become of him. He wouldn't even darken the door of the church, but everybody there was so nice, and they wouldn't say nothing at all about his disfigurement, she knew they wouldn't, not even that Mrs. Casey Hammond, Ota Lee Cagle she'd been when they—she and Miss Maisie--were in school together, and people would treat him just like they always had, just like they had when he was the little eight-year-old boy who'd pulled the preacher down with him when he was baptized in the river. Truth to be told, the river was too high for baptizing that year, but Preacher Armentrough would insist, that's just how he was, and he never did back down from the river later on either, so people took to attending to see if he would get floated away some day, him and the newly baptized soul, if he would waft off to heaven on a wave of holy water.

"But to come back to Matthew, Miss Neville," Miss Maisie concluded, "all the men are going to go looking for him up in the mountains towards that bald where the blackberries come early, but it's much too early for the blackberries up that high, in my opinion. They're thinking he might have intended to hunt squirrels, taking his daddy's rifle like that, or just to be on the watch for boars, you know."

I did not think Matthew was going to hunt blackberries, or squirrels, or even boars. Matthew had been a student in my class only four years ago, and I had a bad, bad feeling about what that rifle said.

As I walked home from the hotel, I saw the men gathering up in the town square to go looking for Matthew. Where might he go? By the time I got home, I had a notion where that might be, and that notion was scarier than the first thing that might come to mind when a soul-wounded young man lit out with a weapon in his hand.

Matthew was where I thought he might be. At what we called the Cliff on the valley side of Tank Hill, a place I'd taken classes to sketch on occasion. It wasn't much of a cliff really, but it was high enough to see a panoramic view of the valley--a flat area called the Blakely Bottoms because that was where Blakely's cannery was situated to handle the crops they'd planted there: corn, peas, and beans. All were now getting to be a healthy size in June.

But there at the edge of the fields was the new German prisoner of war camp, a stockade, I guess you'd call it, a double fence around the perimeter, electrified too, they said. Inside, structures laid out in neat rows and grids. About 150 prisoners were there. They'd been brought in to work at the Blakely Cannery and some of the bigger farms because there was a manpower shortage what with so many local boys being in the service.

On the far side of the bean fields, where the ground sloped up, Kinzell Mansion was just visible through the trees. Kinzell was one of the original lumber men who'd arrived in the 1890s and brought the first economic boom to Settico Plains. That also meant electricity arrived here before some other places in the county. Blakely Cannery had brought more prosperity in the 1920s. The 1930s, however, had slowed down the lumber work. The easier tracts of woods had been cleared out, and much of the remaining mountain land was being considered for the national park or forest. The cannery continued at a slower pace in the 1930s too. Still, all things considered, things had gone well. And now the war had brought a renewed demand for timber and for canned goods. Blakely had a contract to produce food for the army, so when they'd needed more manpower to plant and harvest the crops, the government had responded, much to the surprise of the Settico Plainsmen, by sending us German prisoners of war.

Heated discussion had ensued about that decision. But one of the ironies was that the original lumber men, like Kinzell and Lintz and Sawter, had German roots themselves. They named the company Kinlinsaw. The only hotel in town was the Lintz Hotel, run by the lumber family. Hotel was a little grandiose name for the compact building. "Inn" was more appropriate.

As I got to the edge of the trees when I reached the top of the cliff, several yards ahead of me through the grass and weeds, I saw Matthew's prone body stretched out at the edge of the drop off and thought the worst, but then he slightly shifted his position. I could see that there was a tension about his body, not the relaxation of sleep or death. He was sighting towards the POW camp. He'd remembered the overview of the spot. I feared that he'd come to wreak vengeance in his confusion and anger.

I hesitated, not wanting to startle him but needing to make him aware of my presence.

Before I could give a holler, he called out sharply, "Halt? Who's there?" but he didn't turn from his position of tense vigilance.

"It's Mavis Neville, Matthew." I waited, not knowing what he might do.

"Go away!" he said harshly.

I took a few small steps forward, causing a stick to crack.

He sat up swiftly and turned towards me in a kneeling position. He had enough sense to point the rifle at the ground. After a quick glance to identify me, he lowered his head and turned slightly to the left to conceal his scarred face.

After a pause, he said, "Miss Neville? Well, I'm busy. So leave me alone." He flung himself face on his stomach again to peer over the cliff, rifle in the firing position.

"I came up to sketch," I chattered as if everything were normal, taking a few more steps towards him, brandishing my sketchbook, but he didn't look back at me. "You know I bring my classes up here to sketch, so I like to be familiar with the place. Is it OK if I just sit back here and sketch? I'll be quiet."

"No, no, no," his voice trailed away as if he didn't want to give a reason for his need for solitude.

He won't hurt me, I reassured myself. He was in my class; he knows me.

"Matthew, people are looking for you." I ventured another step closer. "You just disappeared, and they're worried. Your mother's worried."

He made a sound as if something was caught in his throat and startled me by rolling over onto his back but flinging his arm over his face to hide it from me. It was his left arm and the scars on his hand were visible, the ring finger and little finger drawn into a curve by scar tissue. He cleared his throat. The rifle lay to his right, his right arm curving around it. "I remember you bringing us up here."

I shifted my weight, causing a june bug to fly up with its loud buzz, and he called out again, "Stay there, don't come any closer!"

"I won't. I'll stay right here." I sank to the ground and began to sketch as if that were all I wanted to do. He was taut as a bow. A grasshopper sawed away in the weeds close by.

After a moment, as my pencil scratched across the paper like the skittering of a beetle, I said, "What is it, Matthew? Is there something I can do?" I sketched in his outline as he lay there, wrinkled clothes, sweat stains at the neck and arms, right foot trembling slightly.

"No, nothing. I came up here to try out Dad's rifle, to see how it shoots, that's all." His left hand curled into a fist, still hiding most of his face. "When I went into training for the army, they gave us the best rifle. I loved shooting it, taking it apart, cleaning it. It shone like a brand new car. And the smell of that cleaning oil, it was like fresh pepper, it had bite to it, you could just taste it. And you said to yourself, now that's a fine thing. It was just about the prettiest thing I'd ever had. I thought, when this war is over, I want a rifle like this to take home. I wrote Dad all about it."

The air was beginning to bear down with summer's humidity. I tore out a sheet of paper. He flinched at the ripping sound. I said nothing.

I folded the stiff art paper into a fan to cool my face a little and scatter some gnats that had gathered. Setting down the fan, I studied his position again. Because I was on the ground myself, my view was foreshortened, his feet larger and his head smaller than a straight-on view. It reminded me of a painting we'd studied in art school, a strongly foreshortened view of Jesus lying on a table after the crucifixion.

The rifle was not as visible from this perspective. I loosely roughed it in. I paused to think and rolled the pencil between my fingers. Then, balancing the pencil in the relaxed way advocated by my first drawing teacher, I drew long strokes to suggest the grassy, weedy background around Matthew's form, as still as though he were posing for me.

He spoke softly, "*Life* magazine last week—there was this picture—"

I thought I knew the one he was thinking of. *Life* had started to release some of the more gruesome pictures of the battlefront, particularly if they involved the enemy.

"It was a Jap, in a foxhole, dead, from a flamethrower—" he drew in several deep ragged breaths. "They use flamethrowers in Europe, too, at the pillboxes or fortifications. The fire, they shouldn't, fire's not like a bullet, you're marked with it always, and people look at you—" Again several deep breaths. "They tell you you're lucky, you're alive, but here's what I thought, well, if that Jap had survived, and gone home, he'd look worse than me, so it was a good thing he was dead, he'd never have to look at himself in the mirror." He made a sound like a laugh. "Now I'm sympathizing with the enemy."

"I won't tell." I picked up my bag. "I'd like to have a look at the valley. I'm moving closer to the edge, OK?"

He nodded, his hand still over his face, breathing harshly.

Giving him space, I circled him and stopped near a rock. I brushed it off and placed a small towel I'd brought over it. I settled on it and surveyed the valley. Though ringed by steep little hills that marched up to bigger mountains on the east, the valley was as flat as a sheet of green paper except for two little mounds that stuck up in the middle of the green beans and peas. They were Indian mounds. We saw a fair number of them around Settico. I always thought that they needed to be excavated by an archeologist, but they were not very spectacular and seemed too small to be worth anyone's while.

I started outlining the panorama. The prisoners were out hoeing that day. They were spaced ten or eleven to every other row in the green beans. When they got to the end of a row, they'd shift over to the un-hoed row. When they got to the end of that, the whole group of them would walk down to a new set of rows and repeat the process. They looked very ordinary in their work, not the supermen we saw in Nazi propaganda.

I wondered if Matthew's rifle could reach as far as the field they were in.

Matthew remained silent, his breathing slowed, and I almost thought he'd fallen asleep. But his body held a tension still. I wondered what to say to him to try to get him to go peacefully home.

It was a quiet and lovely day with only distant sounds of the Blakely generator running at the cannery, an occasional car engine on the road below, some calls of indistinguishable words among the prisoners and guards, the slam of a door that curiously carried up to us in the wind, and from behind us in the little patch of trees and brush an occasional bird call.

I finished a draft panoramic drawing and turned back to my sketch of Matthew and compared it with the model. Something else struck me about his pose in the drawing, and I couldn't figure out what. I studied him, and then I saw it. His arm over his face like that was almost in the same position as a salute, except for the fact of his curled left hand instead of the stiff, straight right hand. He held a rigid pose although he was lying down. I scrawled "Soldier's Salute" on my sketch.

A blue jay screamed, and simultaneously, there was the sound of someone walking through the brush and trees behind us, where I'd walked from. Matthew reacted by jerking to his knees and bringing up the rifle to point in that direction.

In startlement, I stood up, scattering pencils, sketchbook, and bag.

"Don't move," Matthew ordered. Whether to the one approaching or to me or both, I didn't know, but I froze in place.

Whoever it was kept on coming. "Stop!" Matthew yelled, tightening his grip and raising the rifle to sight the target.

"Who's there?" I shouted. "Wait!"

"I've got this under control. Leave it to me," he said edgily.

The person didn't seem to hear us. His approach continued.

Something awful was going to happen.

"Wait," I said. "Wait, Matthew! Let me see who it is." I stepped forward. Too late.

A black and brown dog stepped out from the brush and stopped to survey us. He was alone.

We were all three surprised.

The blue jay screamed again, and I nearly jumped. A sun ray caught dust motes in the air that swirled for a long minute.

"That's Jose Miller's dog," I said quietly. "Remember? Brownie? That's his name."

Brownie offered a tail wag and sized up the situation.

Matthew slowly lowered the rifle, carefully set it on the ground. He pulled his legs up and circled them with his arms. He rested his forehead on his knees.

Brownie sniffed the air and moseyed forward a few steps.

"Brownie? Here, Brownie!" I held out my hand and snapped my fingers.

Brownie was like a policeman with a beat. Every day, after walking Jose Miller to work at Miller's little grocery store, he'd make his rounds to all of the downtown businesses to check out what was happening, spending more or less time meeting and greeting people, depending on what was going on. Sometimes he'd range up into the neighborhoods, wander by the school, roam through the lumberyard and down to Blakely's fields. Then, in the afternoon, he'd ramble back to the store and flop down under the awning to nap in the shade until it was time for Jose to go home. He was friendly to all except to Miss Maisie and Miss Marnie's cat, a big black and white tomcat who breathed fire and threatenings at other cats, dogs, squirrels, birds, and any squeaky little things he could chase down.

Brownie obliged me by ambling over to be petted. He smelled of something awful. I didn't want to think of what he might have rolled in. "There, there, boy, where in tarnation have you been?"

There was a gulp, maybe a sob, from Matthew, and Brownie pulled away from me to investigate. He sniffed Matthew's sleeve and nudged him with his nose to get his attention. Matthew didn't respond, but his shoulders were shaking. Brownie circled to the other side and tried the same ploy. No response. Brownie butted him with his head.

Matthew opened his arm and pulled him close. Brownie was delighted and rubbed up under his chin, licking his face. The dog wiggled his whole body, his tail thrashing like a propeller. Matthew started coughing. "Phew! Damn! Where've you been, Brownie?" The dog was even more pleased and shoved up against him, knocking him backwards, making it easier to lick his face.

"Brownie, stop that! Back off!" Matthew said, coughing and sneezing. But he was making little effort to escape.

I gathered my pencils and other supplies. I closed my sketch book on the drawing of Matthew. I could not show it to him yet. Maybe at some time further in the future. Or, perhaps, never.

The angle of the light had changed just enough to indicate that the sun was starting to sink.

"Matthew, what do you say that we take Brownie on home?"

Matthew sat up and continued to hang on to the dog. But he didn't stand. He cleared his throat. "Sometimes, Miss Neville, I have these thoughts—I don't know where they come from. And I feel like—I'm not here, like I'm somewhere else." He wiped at his right eye, where there were tears. "Brownie's smell—made my eyes water."

"Me too. What do you think he's been into?"

"No telling. Hold him for a minute so he doesn't knock me

down."

I pulled Brownie away and petted him. I already smelled like he did anyway.

Matthew slowly got to his feet. For the first time he seemed to really look at me. "Good thing you wore pants—you can wash off the smell. You know, you're the first lady I ever saw to wear pants. We didn't know what to think when we saw you." He almost grinned.

"I still get a lot of stares."

Matthew turned away slightly and carefully removed the bullets from the rifle. "Don't want to accidentally shoot old Brownie."

"No." Some pressure eased up in me.

"The nurses, the ones in the field and on the hospital plane, they wore pants too. It's funny looking, but it makes a lot of sense." He looked back at the POW camp. "Sometimes I think I'm—crazy." He glanced quickly at me and then away. "I don't know what I was going to do, Miss Neville. Target practice—or something—"

"But you didn't."

"That picture in the magazine. It all just came over me again like—electricity. I just wanted to do—something. To hurt somebody—something—maybe me." The last words were a whisper.

"You didn't." I assured him gently. "Matthew, let's get Brownie on home so he can get a bath, OK?"

He nodded. Finally.

We started slowly back into town with Brownie happily roaming off to the sides of the path looking for unsuspecting squirrels. He had no luck, however. I guess his odor was as pungent to the squirrels as it was to us.

We talked about nothing very serious on the way back—mostly other dogs Matthew had had. We didn't encounter any of the other searchers on the way back. They'd all gone in the other direction towards the mountains.

When we stopped in front of Matthew's house, I saw his mother watching from the window. She vanished. I knew she would be out the door in a minute.

"Matthew, I know you'll be going away for some more treatments, but while you're here, if you ever want to talk, I'd be glad to listen."

He nodded and permitted himself a small smile. "Thank you,

Miss Neville. I always liked your drawing classes. Remember when we made the kites?" For a moment, he looked boyish again, despite the scars. I remembered him and his best friend, Louie, competing to fly their kites the highest, dashing across the football field.

Mrs. Hawkins was out the door, running towards us. "Matthew, oh, Matthew!"

"See who I ran into, Mrs. Hawkins," I said.

She embraced him and clung to him. "Oh, thank you, Miss Neville! Thank you!" Her focus shifted to Matthew. "Now, you'll be hungry, son. Let's get you some supper." Brownie gamboled around them as they walked to the house in a whirl of her relief and love and, as the door closed, her saying, "what's that smell?"

Brownie realized that he was not going to be included in the welcome, so he rejoined me and escorted me until we went by Jose's house where he trotted up to the porch and flopped down.

I couldn't get Matthew and the boys from my classes out of my mind. I saw them chasing across the football field with their kites. Now most of them were scattered around the world. I thought about the sketch I'd made of Matthew. There would be other Matthews.

A few days later, after consulting with Mrs. Hawkins, I brought Matthew a puppy. Mrs. McCall's dog had had puppies a few weeks back. Matthew seemed very pleased, relaxing to sit on the floor to submit to the eager wiggling of the tan puppy. It had a white splotch on its face and four uneven white socks on its legs.

"He'll take some schooling." He rubbed the puppy's stomach.

"I bet," I replied. Mrs. Hawkins smiled at me.

The little dog had a job too: to coax Matthew to outside again, outside his house, and outside himself.

I had confidence in both.

Thursday Morning

Will Martin

Brown, blue, and green, in a straight line they stand.
In the dark void between their broad shoulders,
How discreetly and how humbly they hold
The smelly and shameful dross of our lives.
They are remarkable, perfectly fit
To reach the purpose of their creation,
Their reason for being so manifest.
I take them on their journey down the drive,
And next morning I listen for the sounds
Of the fierce purging of all that's in them
By the brawny arms of big rumbling trucks.

Some days I'd like to be a rollout cart,
To know beyond any doubt why I'm here,
To be wholly emptied from time to time.

Migratory

Mark MacAllister

— Pocosin Lakes National Wildlife Refuge

Snow geese   tundra swans
    green-winged teal
overwinter here
they rest and eat and mate
in loud uncountable crowds

this started long before anyone
took it upon himself
to label these lakes *refuge*

today's birds pass directly overhead
you watch them through your windshield
as you move west toward a new home

as I would not presume to suggest
where you might land safely
or how best to seek others of your kind

I will instead wish for you
a wall of east-facing windows
dark wood floors warmed
    by new ragg rugs

space enough to run a big dumb dog or two

an upstairs bedroom door that clicks
    itself closed
once the sweet-scented crossbreezes
arrive in the spring

The Hammer

Bryant Vielman

"That was fun. Thank you," she said tentatively as the car gradually made its way down Fourth Street. They passed couples walking in the night holding hands, and restaurants busy with romantic dinners underway: dim lighting and tables adorned with roses. She looked at him and smiled meekly.

"Thank you for agreeing," he replied, "I enjoyed myself."

The politeness in their tone betrayed restraint and a fragile newly-formed peace. Every word was measured, calculated. Despite their cautious interaction, the conversation over dinner had been relaxed and comforting in its familiarity. At different moments they both felt acute feelings of nostalgia—momentary slips in time, five years back, laughing freely, energy high. The night was a success after months of constant bickering, volatile drunken calls, and shouting matches, so you couldn't blame them for greeting the current pleasantry with open—if careful—arms. They made a right on Cherry Street and as it merged onto University Parkway, they nestled and dropped their defenses.

"Did you like my dress?"

"I do like it. You look great."

"You didn't say anything."

"I don't want to be overwhelming. I already worried that dinner and flowers might be too much too soon."

He wondered if she noticed this subtle change in behavior. She offered nothing in response, but instead looked out at the blurring trees. She spoke:

"You know, the other day I was with friends and uploaded a selfie of the outfit I was wearing to Instagram. I felt so pretty. I posted a sticker on it that read, *'You were saying?'*"

She let it linger. The air hung heavy with implication—with indignation. He became tense.

"You really hurt me," she added. Her words stung.

"I know. I'm truly sorry. But you know I meant none of it. You know how I feel. I was hurt."

A long silence ensued in which he debated continuing this thread. He recalled an adage he'd been mulling over for months, an adage he'd personalized: *If all you have in your relational toolbox is a hammer, you'll treat everyone like a nail.* He decided to proceed—his tone conversational.

"I'm hurt too. There are words I replay in my head as well, but I don't publicly post passive-aggressive messages for the world to decipher."

"I'm not posting passive-aggressive messages for anyone," she retorted. "I'm just reminding myself of something. I'm going out and dressing the way I want to prove a point."

An exercise in restraint: he said nothing. After another awkward pause, she decided to change the course she'd set.

"Can we talk about something else? I don't want to ruin the night like this."

And so, they spoke of other things—random tidbits to fill the rest of the car ride with and the momentary tension quickly dissolved itself. He pulled into her driveway and killed the engine. Her hand in his, he led the way up, his feet tracing a familiar path out of habit to her front door. He suggested they hang out again.

"I want to hang out, but I don't want to agree every time you suggest it. What if we end up bickering like we just did?" She anticipated a reaction, but when none came, she added, "Can I think about it?"

She was anxious. He sensed it.

"It's ok," he said and moved closer, "I understand. Let's not worry about it right now."

He hugged her and returned to his car. Within minutes of leaving her neighborhood, his phone pinged with a notification—a text from her: *You give up so easily.* He wondered for the second time that night if she'd even noticed.

Flying South 2024 Editors

Mary Hennessy (Poetry Editor): Mary was a registered nurse most of her adult life. She returned to school late and fell in with a community of generous, word-crazed people. Her poems have appeared in many journals and anthologies. She is a Pushcart nominee. Poetry is the only thing that makes sense to her anymore.

Jennifer Stevenson Vincent (Creative Nonfiction Editor): Jennifer was twice nominated for the Pulitzer Prize with a specialty in Civil Rights issues. She has a distinguished career in print journalism, including senior staff writer at the *St. Petersburg (Fla.) Times*. A founder and past President of Winston-Salem Writers, she's taught creative non-fiction at New York University, the University of South Florida and Salem College.

Howard Pearre (Fiction Editor): Howard's stories have appeared in *Daniel Boone Footsteps* anthologies, *Flying South, GreenPrints,* and *The Dead Mule School of Southern Literature*. He writes articles promoting voting for the Winston-Salem Chronicle. Howard retired after a career as a counselor and manager with NC Vocational Rehabilitation and the US Department of Veterans Affairs.

Joni Carter (Fiction Reader): Joni's fiction has been published in online and print journals Her nonfiction work has appeared in *Our State* and in the *Greensboro News and Record* (Rockingham County edition). She has won a number of local writing awards and is also an avid reader. When she's driving Joni loves listening to audiobooks. She enjoys character driven stories, especially the fun ones.

Ray Morrison (Fiction Reader): Ray is an award-winning writer whose stories have appeared in numerous journals and magazines, including *Ecotone, Carve, Beloit Fiction Journal,* and *Fiction Southeast*. He is the author of the story collections, *In a World of Small Truths*

(Press 53) and *I Hear the Human Noise* (Press 53). *I Hear the Human Noise* was awarded the 2020 IPPY Gold Medal for Southeast – Best Regional Fiction.

Steve Lindahl (Fiction Reader): Steve is the author of eight novels, *Motherless Soul* (ATTMP), *White Horse Regressions* (ATTMP), *Hopatcong Vision Quest* (Solstice), *Under a Warped Cross* (Solstice), *Living in a Star's Light* (Self Published), *Chasing Margie* (Solstice), *Woodstock to St. Joseph's* (Solstice), and *Ginger's Shoes* (Self Published). His short fiction has appeared in *The Alaska Quarterly*, *The Wisconsin Review*, *Eclipse* and others. He served for five years on the staff of *The Crescent Review* and is the current Managing Editor of *Flying South*. (www.stevelindahl.com)

Contributors

Richard Band: Richard is a retired librarian and trustee of the Arras Foundation in Lancaster, South Carolina. His work has appeared in *South Carolina Review*, *Kakalak*, *Poetry South*, *Main Street Rag*, *Whimsical Poet*, and elsewhere. He collects the works of Irish writer Padraic Colum and sometimes reads them. A poem, he believes with Robert Frost, is "a momentary stay against confusion."

Jenny Bates: Jenny has seven poetry books, published in numerous NC and international journals. She presented at the 2023 Ecopoetics and Environmental Aesthetics Conference, London. Jenny was a judge for the *Poetry in Plain Sight* contest through the NC Poetry Society, 2024. Her book of poems, *ESSENTIAL*, Redhawk Publications 2023 has been nominated for the Pushcart Prize 2024. Her newest collection, *From Soil and Soul* is available through Redhawk Publications. Jenny's books are also available at Malaprops Bookstore in Asheville, Bookmarks, the Book Ferret and The Book House in Winston-Salem, Scuppernongs in Greensboro, NC.

Mason Boyles: Mason is a teacher, Youtuber, podcaster, and author. His first novel, *Bark On*, was nominated for the Pulitzer, and his award-winning short fiction has been nominated for the Pushcart Prize. He holds his M.F.A. from UC-Irvine and his Ph.D. from Florida State. You can find him on Youtube at @storiedstrength. He is currently seeking an agent for his steampunk Western, *The Voidheart Engine*. Find out more about his writing and teaching at masonboylesauthor.com.

Hugh Burke: Hugh is a public school educator and poet living in central Texas. Drawing from a keen adoration and attention to the natural world along with a sincere scrutiny of experience, his poems have been described as ethereal, disarming, and stark. Hugh's work has received awards and publication in the *Texas Poetry Society Anthology*, *Waco Wordfest Anthology*, *Living Peace Anthology* and *Texas*

Marie Chambers: Marie is a Southerner by birth and an Angelino by choice. Her work has appeared in *The LA Review of Books. The Atlanta Review, Talking Writing, The Quotable, Ilanot Review, Printer's Devil Review, Ironhorse Literary Review* and *The Writer.* She was a winner of *ARTlines2 Ekphrasic Poetry Contest* judged by Robert Pinsky. Her writing has been published in numerous art catalogues and her collaboration with Paris-based visual artist Daniela Bershon was featured in the online magazine *"7 x 7."* She has an MFA in Poetry from Bennington College and most recently was a finalist for the *Lascaux Poetry Prize.*

Morrow Dowdle: Morrow has poetry published in or forthcoming from *New York Quarterly, Baltimore Review, Ghost City Review,* and *Fatal Flaw Literary Magazine,* among others. They have been nominated for the Pushcart Prize and Best of the Net, and were a finalist in the *Flying South* contest in 2023. They edit poetry for *Sunspot Literary Journal* and run a performance series called *"Weave & Spin"* featuring underrepresented voices. They live in Hillsborough, NC.

Rick Forbess: Rick is a seventy-six-year-old writer with eleven published short fiction pieces. His wife, daughter, and he migrated from Texas to Maine almost four decades ago, and here they happily remain. Since retirement from a long career in the mental health field, he has read more, written more, and worked on refining how to approach both.

Charles Gammon: For the past two years Charles has worked in higher education, and this year will begin a master's degree program with a concentration in literary studies. Most of his writing is an attempt to capture moments in everyday observations or experiences, as well as general complexities of human life, America, and diverse parts of history. He enjoys reading Whitman, Proust, Dumas, Limón, and Faulkner.

Shannon Golden: Shannon's publication history includes only scientific and technical writing, related to a career in research. As an emerging creative writer, she is focusing her talents on flash fiction and creative nonfiction. She is a member of Winston-Salem Writers and, until recently, never knew a critique group could be so much fun.

Vera Guertler: Both poets and physicians catalyze change. Vera's poetry reflects engagement with survivors of domestic violence, suicide, and immigration. Such experiences have led to publishing in *Pivot, Wild Onions, Scope,* and bilingual magazines. Her preceptorship with medical students, ER work with First Americans on a reservation, and medical volunteering overseas have led to published journal essays. She believes intertwining creativity with critical inquiry generates healing individually and collectively.

Emily Hall: Emily is a freelance writer with a PhD in English from the University of North Carolina at Greensboro. Her creative nonfiction has appeared in *Taproot Magazine, Pedagogy,* and *The AutoEthnographer,* and her micro-nonfiction has appeared in *TheKeepthings.* She lives in Greensboro, North Carolina with her husband and two pets.

Mike Herndon: Mike is a former journalist who earned an MA in Creative Writing from the University of South Alabama and now teaches future journalists there that past-tense verbs are their friends. His fiction has appeared in *South 85, Blue Mountain Review, Book of Matches, Change Seven* and elsewhere, along with the Mobile Writers Guild's latest anthology, *Classic Pieces Retold.*

John J. Hohn: John grew up in the Midwest and graduated from St. John's University (MN) in 1961. In 2007, he retired at the age of 68 closing out a career of more than 40 years in the financial services industry. His published works include two novels and a random poem or two. He is the co-founder of 40+ Stage Company and has appeared frequently on stage over the past 40 years with local community theater companies. He and his wife Melinda reside in Winston-Salem. His five children and stepson are spread far and wide across the country.

Karen Luke Jackson: Karen's poems have appeared in *Atlanta Review, EcoTheo Review, Susurrus, Friends Journal, and Salvation South*, among others. Winner of the Rash Poetry Award and a Pushcart Prize nominee, she has also authored three poetry collections: *If You Choose To Come* (2023), *The View Ever Changing* (2021), and *GRIT* (2020). Karen resides in a cottage on a goat pasture in the Blue Ridge Mountains where she writes and companions people on their spiritual journeys.

CM Kelly: With two engineering degrees, CM Kelly's passion has always been focused on numbers, formulas and equations. Raised as the fourth of nine children, his household was rich in character, though light on finances. Hard work and laughter were constants. In many ways, it was akin to a *Waltons* setting with a touch of Archie Bunker. Now retired, he enjoys writing about his life experiences that range from; growing up in a large family, working in the coal mines to building billion-dollar projects.

Karen Bryant Lucas: Karen is a writer and retired church musician. Having spent most of her life in the church, either as the daughter of a Baptist preacher, or as an organist and choral director, in retirement she prefers to spend her days reading, drinking lattes (whole milk, please), and considering the lilies of the field. At the age of 69, Karen fell in love with a man she met more than half a century ago. Now a newlywed, she lives in Wake Forest, NC, with her husband William, for whom she delights in baking a wickedly delicious cheesecake in the slowcooker.

Carol Luther: Carol has published fiction in *The Notebook: A Progressive Journal about Women & Girls with Rural & Small Town Roots, Still: The Journal, Persimmon Tree, Broad River Review* and elsewhere. She is professor emerita at Pellissippi State Community College in

Knoxville, TN, where she taught literature, writing, and film studies.

Mark MacAllister: Mark grew up in Illinois, spent a great deal of formative time on his grandparents' dairy farm in southwest Wisconsin's Driftless region, and learned to write at Oberlin College. Mark now lives in Pittsboro, North Carolina but travels often to the Wisconsin Northwoods and to Michigan's Upper Peninsula to hike the backcountry. His poems appear in various journals, including *"Steam Ticket," "Quiet Diamonds," "The Journal of Undiscovered Poets," "Deep Wild: Writing From the Backcountry," "Moss Piglet"* and *"Passager Journal."* Mark's chapbook, *"Quiet Men And Their Coyotes,"* won the 2022 Concrete Wolf Chapbook Contest and was published in January 2023.

Will Martin: Will is married, the father of three, and a retired lawyer. His interests include reading, writing, cycling, golf, and yard work.

Barbara Rizza Mellin (cover artist): Barbara is a painter/printmaker, and poet. As an art historian, she loves reinterpreting traditional techniques for contemporary audiences. Mellin's art has appeared in galleries, universities and museums, and in juried exhibitions throughout the US and internationally online. She lives with her husband in a Philadelphia suburb. www.BarbaraRizzaMellin.com

Susan Woods Morse: Susan lives in Oregon. Her chapbook, *In the Hush,* was published June 2019 by Finishing Line Press. She is a previous board member of the Oregon Poetry Association. Poems have appeared in various journals such as *Cirque, Verseweavers, Literary Mama, The Poeming Pigeon, Aji Magazine,* and *Willawaw Journal.*

Rebecca Petzel: Rebecca is a co-founder of the Emergence Collective, a collaborative consulting firm working to find better ways to tackle our most pressing societal challenges. She is also the proud and recovering mom of a NICU survivor. She lives in

Chicago, IL with her husband, two kids, and wild cattle-dog mutt named Winter

Nancy Werking Poling: Nancy is the author of *"While Earth Still Speaks,"* an environmental novel, and *"Before It Was Legal: a black-white marriage (1945-1987),"* non-fiction. She has contributed to numerous anthologies, most recently *"Wholeness"* (Wising Up Press, 2023); *"Wild Crone Wisdom"* (Wild Librarian Press, 2023); and *"County Lines"* (Vol. 11-2024). She maintains a website at https://nancypoling.com and posts on Facebook and Instagram. She lives in the North Carolina mountains.

Joyce Schmid: Joyce's work has appeared or is forthcoming in *Bridport Prize Anthology 2023, The Hudson Review, Five Points, Literary Imagination, New Ohio Review, Antioch Review, Poetry Daily, Missouri Review,* and other journals and anthologies. She lives in Palo Alto, California, with her husband of over half a century.

Richard Allen Taylor: Richard (Greer, SC) is the author of four books of poetry, most recently *Letters to Karen Carpenter and Other Poems* (Main Street Rag Publishing Company, 2023). Taylor's poems, articles and reviews have appeared in *Rattle, Comstock Review, The Pedestal, Iodine Poetry Journal, Running with Water, Wild Goose Poetry Review, Asheville Poetry Review, Litmosphere,* and *South Carolina Review,* among others. A Pushcart Prize nominee, Taylor formerly served as review editor for The Main Street Rag and co-editor of *Kakalak*. He earned an MFA in Creative Writing from Queens University of Charlotte in 2015.

Claire Thomas: Claire is a nonfiction and travel writer living in the mountains of Western North Carolina. When not scribbling down her latest story, Claire can be found antiquing, drinking a glass of red wine on her porch, or researching her next off-the-beaten-path destination.

Bryant Vielman: Bryant is a writer and poet of Guatemalan descent. A New York City native, he now lives in North Carolina where he reads and writes as often as he can. He began writing poetry seven years ago and saw publication in the Winter issue of *"The Raven Review"*, published in January of 2024.

Robert Wallace: Robert is a two-time winner of the *Doris Betts Fiction Contest*. His short story collection *As Breaks the Wave Upon the Sea* was published by the Main Street Publishing Company in 2021. His work has been published in the *NC Literary Review, the Bryant Literary Review*, and *The Petigru Review*, among others. He can be followed at https://www.robertwallaceauthor.com/ and on Instagram @robertwallacewriter.

Emily Wilson: Emily is a writer of coming-of-age and contemporary fiction. She is currently unpublished. When she's not busy writing, Wilson works full-time as a mental health counselor for children and teens.